PRAIS

MW00466285

"This is dark stuff, but fun, without any hipster wink of irony or cynicism. Writing stories that are simultaneously grim and good-hearted is a fucking tough line to straddle, and writing them well... let's just say I don't see that often. Chaplinsky walks a barbed-wire tightrope here. In short, good shit."

— CRAIG CLEVENGER, AUTHOR OF
CONTORTIONIST HANDBOOK

"Spend some time in Chaplinsky's weird and wild stories and you may want to bathe afterward, but you will have been relentlessly entertained."

— KELLY THOMPSON, EISNER
NOMINATED WRITER OF DEADPOOL,
CAPTAIN MARVEL, X-MEN

"In Whispers in the Ear of a Dreaming Ape, Joshua Chaplinsky takes readers on a wild ride through a landscape of darkness and absurdity. You may think yourself safe, but you'll learn soon enough—no one rides for free."

— KEVIN KOLSCH, WRITER/DIRECTOR
OF STARRY EYES, PET SEMATARY

"The weird tales of Joshua Chaplinsky are full of magic and surprises. Whispers In the Ear of a Dreaming Ape is one of the most original short story collections of the year. A must-read if you like your fiction smart and strange."

— CAMERON PIERCE, AUTHOR OF OUR
LOVE WILL GO THE WAY OF THE
SALMON

"If you're sick of tepid short stories that taste like watered down milk, "Whispers in the Ear of a Dreaming Ape," is the collection of multi-colored, bite-sized brain pan bullets that might just be the cure. Joshua Chaplinsky has an imagination both of depth and breadth, and no two stories are alike. You can practically hear the lively, fascinating, hallucinatory click of his brain throughout the book. An enjoyable read for all of us dreaming apes."

— AUTUMN CHRISTIAN, AUTHOR OF
GIRL LIKE A BOMB

WHISPERS IN THE EAR OF A DREAMING APE

JOSHUA CHAPLINSKY

CL4SH

For my father,

who never even got the chance to have his foot amputated once.

CONTENTS

LETTERS TO THE PURPLE SATIN KILLER

Dear Jonas Williker,

My name is Ginny Goodwinch, and I'm a single mother of two from Chappaqua New York. (Bobby is five and Little Derrik is three. Mommy loves you!) I've been following your case and I must confess, I find it hard to believe a man with such a kind face could do those horrible things. It's like my momma always says, kind face, gentle heart. Of course, Momma thinks you're guilty as heck, but you can't be right all the time.

The reporter on the news said you didn't have much family, so I figured you might need someone to talk to. It must get lonely in solitary confinement, even if it is for your own safety. I know what it's like to be lonely. Sometimes you can be surrounded by people and still feel like the only human being on the planet.

Anyway, feel free to write me back. You can't believe everything you hear on TV, and I'd love to get to know the real you.

Sincerely,

Ginny Goodwinch

———

Dear Jonas,

How are you holding up? Are they feeding you enough? I know prison can be tough. Your father and I have been watching that television series, the Oz one? I don't like all the cussing and the violence, but I want to stay informed about your situation. I don't know if you are aware of this, but there are men that dress like ladies in there, so be careful. Can you believe such a thing?

Oh. Your father just reminded me that one of your alleged victims was a he-she. I'm sure you didn't realize it was a man.

Speaking of your father, he's still pretty upset about the whole situation. I'll try to get him on the phone next time you call, but no promises. You know how stubborn he can be. I'm sure he didn't mean those things he said, about you burning in hell and whatnot. No matter what you've done, you're still our son. Dad's just never been very good at handling his emotions.

I'll write again soon.

Love,
Mom

———

Dear Purple,

You make my cunt ache. I want to turn it inside out so you can carve your name into it. I want to slather you in my pussy juice and watch the jury lick it off. Make me your fuck slave.

xoxo,
Staci

———

Dear Jonas Williker,

I was so happy to get your letter! I've never had a penpal before!

Of course I'll tell you a little more about myself. I'm twenty-nine years old (I've been twenty-nine for the last thirteen years now!), and I've lived in Chappaqua all my life. I married right out of high school, which I do NOT recommend, and worked part-time as a bookkeeper for the local lumber yard. My husband Ronnie was a drinker, and what momma used to call a "cooze hound." He took off right before I turned twenty-nine for the second time. We never had any kids, and the single life hasn't been easy, what with my thyroid issues. So a few years ago I adopted Bobby and Derrik, two special needs children. (The approval process is faster for specials, because no one wants them.) They bring so much sunshine into my otherwise dreary life!

But listen to me, complaining! How are things with you? Is your arm feeling any better? I can't believe they let that guard get away with such cruelty. Even if you did threaten to violate the stump of his mother's headless corpse (which I know you didn't). What's this world coming to?

I'm enclosing a picture of myself, as requested. It's a few years old, but I don't really have a lot of photos without the kids. I hope you don't mind that I'm only wearing a night-gown. I think I look really pretty in it. (Now I'm blushing!)

Anyway, I never had anyone to share it with, so I hope you like it.

Your pal,
Ginny

———

Dear Jonas,

I hate to be the bearer of bad news, but your father isn't doing so well. The press has been hounding him non-stop and the stress is really getting to him. He can't even go out to get the paper without someone shoving a camera "in his face." (I've toned down his colorful language, just in case anyone else is reading these letters.) He's also taken to drinking again, and you know how bad that is for his IBS. Plus, with my arthritis, I can't scrub a toilet the way I used to.

Personally, I don't mind the press. You just need to talk to them like regular people. One time they even put me on the news! I told them all about what a smart, well-behaved kid you were. I felt like a star! Unfortunately your father wasn't too happy about it, so now I'm not allowed to talk to them. It's a shame, because your father isn't much of a conversationalist these days.

Have you made any friends on the inside? It's always good to have someone to watch your back!

Love you,
Mom

———

Dear Purple,

I want you to tie me up and bathe in my menstrual blood. I want to feel the knife you used to cut them moving inside me. How much longer will you make me wait? I've rubbed my pussy raw reading the autopsy reports.

xoxo,
Staci

———

Jonas,

Just a reminder, please exercise discretion when corresponding with members of the public. As you should be well aware, the correctional facility inspects all inmate mail, and anything you commit to writing may be used against you in court. Try to keep this in mind as your trial approaches. As your attorney, I would recommend suspending all non-essential communication with the outside world. It can only make my job more difficult.

Anita Trellis, Esq.

———

Dear Mr. Williker,

My name is Candace Bennington. I am a PhD student in the Criminal Justice program at John J. University, and I have a proposition for you. Undoubtedly your legal team has counseled you against giving any interviews until after the trial, but I am not interested in the specifics of your legal woes. I am interested in your perspective.

I am writing my Thesis on the phenomenon of Hybristophilia, commonly referred to as "Bonnie and Clyde Syndrome." Basically, it is a term used to describe a person who is sexually attracted to criminals (or those who are perceived as such, as may be your case). Based on what I'm seeing in the news, this is an area in which you have some experience. It has been reported that you receive quite a bit of fan mail, and that attendance at your pre-trial hearings has been predominantly female.

I would love to set up a time to speak with you, if you would be amenable. Please let me know at your earliest convenience.

Sincerely,
Candace Bennington

———

Dear Jonas Williker,

Allow me to introduce myself. My name is Abigail Tinder, and I am a twelve-year-old preacher's daughter from Argos, Indiana. I am writing to tell you that even though you are a despicable sinner who has committed heinous crimes, it is not too late to save your soul from eternal damnation.

Of course, fear of hell is not, in and of itself, a valid justification for redemption. I had to learn that lesson the hard way. As it says in the book of Romans, you must renounce your sin, and believe with all your heart that Jesus Christ is Lord. Only then can you truly be saved.

It is that easy.

If you are interested, I have enclosed a tract with a simple sinner's prayer for you to recite. I am also available to further instruct you in the ways of righteousness. I believe your conversion would be a valuable testimony to the saving grace of our Lord Jesus Christ (not that he needs it, mind you). You could be the next David Berkowitz. Think about it.

Yours in Christ,
Abigail Tinder

———

Dear Jonas,

I saw you on the television today. You looked so handsome in your suit! Was it my imagination or were there an awful lot of women in the courtroom? You better not be cheating on me! (Just kidding.)

Speaking of kids, Bobby and Derek have been driving me up the wall. (You hear me, guys? Mommy's still very upset about her Kristi Yamaguchi commemorative plates!) Sometimes I feel like they're the only thing holding me back from driving across the country to visit you. Would you like that? I'd leave the kids with Momma, but she's been confined to that dang wheelchair ever since she broke her hip. (She doesn't think I know, but EMS told me she was fornicating with the gardener in the shower when it happened!)

Sometimes I get so angry over the things they say about you on the news. What happened to innocent until proven guilty? They don't know you raped and murdered all those women. That's for the jury to decide. I wish I knew where that mean old news anchor lived, I would drive to her house and give her a piece of my mind!

Love you,
Ginny

———

Dear Jonas,

I know you have a lot going on with your trial, and I hate to be a bother, but I have to ask. Do you remember your

cousin Tina? You were only five or six at the time, but she
went missing during the family picnic that year. We
searched the woods for days and never found any trace of
her—which is why your Aunt Lottie had to go live at the
hospital for a while. Then a few weeks later, I found her
jacket in the back of your closet. The purple one, with the
white trim? It was all torn up and stained, and when I asked
you how it got there you just shrugged and gave me that
blank stare, the one you made in all your school pictures.
I'm not accusing you of anything, but the purple satin used
to gag your alleged victims reminded me of that jacket. All I
know is that even after all these years, it would be a real
relief for Aunt Lottie to know what happened to poor Tina.

On a lighter note, I saw that news piece about all your lady-
admirers. Your father nearly fell out of his chair, but I'm not
surprised. You can be quite the charmer when you put your
mind to it. Remember the time Mrs. Edmunds was going to
give you a B+ on that paper, and you convinced her to give
you an A? She told me you made a very compelling case and
she just couldn't say no. I was so proud!

Love you,
Mom

———

Dear Mr. Williker

Thank you for your timely response. I will get right to the
point by saying I appreciate the concerns you have. So, as
requested, here is a little more about me and my project.

You are correct in assuming my interest in this subject
matter stems from personal experience. You see, I never
knew my father. He was a career criminal who spent the
entirety of my childhood behind bars. My mother, in her
infinite wisdom, never allowed me to visit him. By the time

I was old enough to do so on my own, he was dead. Stabbed in the throat by a jagged piece of lunch tray. It was over a fruit cup.

Despite depriving me of a personal relationship with my own father, my mother corresponded with him often. It drove a wedge between us. This project is partly an attempt to understand her motivation. How could she be so obsessed with a man she professed to hate? Was she just trying to protect me from him? Or was she trying to keep him all to herself?

I hope this has satisfied your curiosity. Please let me know if we could meet.

Sincerely,
Candace Bennington

———

Dear Jonas,

I wish I could have seen what you did to their bodies. Tell me, did you fuck them before or after you cut their eyes out? Which one was your favorite? Was it Glenda Myers? Or was it Stefanie Kellerman? I'll bet it was Stefanie. The autopsy report said you dug up her body days later to go back for seconds. Remember how her husband broke down when he found out? It was deliciously pathetic. She must have been one sweet peach.

Would you like to do those things to me?

xoxo
Staci

———

Mr. Williker,

I represent a contingent of concerned bereaved looking only for closure. It is a well known fact that there are many missing and presumed dead associated with your case that have yet to be recovered. You hinted at as much yourself during your police interrogation, which is part of the public record. Maybe you were only toying with them, but I do not believe that to be the case. If you have any humanity left, I implore you, please release the details and locations of all your victims so their families can say goodbye properly. It would be an act of kindness on your part.

Sincerely,
Aurelius Percy, Esq.
Percy, Paramount & Bint

———

Dear Jonas,

It's been a while since I've heard from you. Is everything okay? Why haven't you written me back? If this is about the woman who flashed her breasts in the courtroom, don't worry—I'm not mad at you. I know it's not your fault women are attracted to you. They see you as a hunter, an alpha male. It's only natural. Just please, write back soon. I know I get to see your face on TV every day, but your words bring me so much comfort. Whenever I get a letter from you I turn on Court TV and turn the volume down, so I can read it out loud and pretend you're talking to me. Of course, it breaks my concentration when they cut to that ugly old judge, and the children don't understand that sometimes mommy needs "private time," but it's all I have. Please. Just thinking about it makes me burn inside!

I've enclosed another snapshot as an incentive. It's a bit naughty, so don't let the guards see. I had my Bobby take it.

For a little guy, he's pretty good with the camera! Anyway, there's plenty more where that came from.

Love and kisses,
Your Ginny Bird

———

Dear Mr. Williker

I appreciate you taking the time to speak with me last week. It was very enlightening. In fact—and please do not take this the wrong way—I must admit that you were not at all what I expected. I was impressed with how intelligently you spoke on the subjects of criminal justice and psychology. Do you have a background in law enforcement?

Regardless, I am in your debt. The insights you provided will make a great addition to my dissertation, as will the interviews I conducted with your so-called groupies. They are quite a possessive bunch. It wasn't easy to convince them my interests in you were strictly academic. Good thing I am a skilled liar.

Would it be possible to set up another meeting? I have some...follow-up questions.

Yours,
Candace Bennington

———

Mr. Jonas Williker,

I have yet to receive a response from you, which leads me to believe one of two things:

You believe you deserve hell. If that is the case, let me

remind you that we ALL deserve hell. It is only by the blood
of Christ, his sacrifice in our stead, that we are washed clean
of sin and permitted entry into the gates of heaven. The
egregious nature of your crimes aside, there is very little
difference between you and I.

Either that, or you are a prideful man who takes pleasure
from spitting in the face of God. Such defiance can only
result in destruction. Proverbs chapter 16, verse 5 says:
Everyone who is arrogant in heart is an abomination to the
Lord; be assured, he will not go unpunished.

Do you think you are too good for the grace of God? You
will burn in hell for your arrogance, along with all the unre-
pentant fags and baby-killers. Consider yourself warned.

Yours in Christ,
Abigail Tinder

———

Alright, Buster,

I don't know who this Candace slut is or what kind of spell she's
got you under, but I will tear her fucking eyes out. Imagine my
surprise when I turned on the TV, all set to read your latest
letter and get a little well-deserved alone time with my man,
only to hear you propose to some random bitch in open court!
Are you doing this to spite me? Is it because I couldn't be there
with you? Well guess what? I left the kids at Mom's while she
was sleeping, and by the time you read this I will be halfway
across the country on my way to the courthouse.

Do you think this whore knows you like I know you? Do
you think she sees through all the fame and the bullshit to
the vulnerable person you really are? I was there for you
when no one else was. I don't care if you did kill all those

people, you have brought so much joy into my life, and I am not about to let that go. So you tell this piece of trash I'm coming for her, and if she's still around when I get there, I'm going to destroy her world.

Your future wife,
Mrs. Ginny Williker

————

Dear Purple,

I took these pictures of my pussy for you. They are part of a larger series based on your life's work. I consider them my crowning achievement as an artist and a monument to your greatness.

Do they have the Internet in jail? If so, you can see more at my personal website, stacixxx.com. Maybe you could mention it the next time the cameras are rolling. I could use the hits.

I probably won't be able to write for a while, as money's getting tight and I have to work all the time. Plus, my manager is kind of the jealous type. But if my website takes off and I'm able to pay him the money I owe him, there'll be nothing left standing between us.

xoxo
Staci

————

Dear Jonas,

You've certainly had an exciting week! I couldn't believe my eyes when they showed that mad woman on the courthouse steps, screaming bloody murder. What is this world coming to? I hope that poor reporter she bit is okay.

And congratulations on the engagement! I must admit, I wasn't sure what to think at first. I was as shocked as anyone when you proposed, but Candy seems like she's a good fit for you. You need a smart woman to take care of you after your mother's gone. It just goes to show, it's never too late to turn things around. You might make a grandma out of me yet!

Unfortunately, I also have some bad news. Your father is in the hospital. He didn't take too well to the news of your engagement. In fact, he got so worked up he burst a blood vessel in his head. I know you two never really got along, but please keep him in your prayers.

Love always,
Mom

———

To My Dearest Jonas,

I don't know if you've heard the news, but I went and got myself arrested. Now don't you worry, they're treating me just fine. I'm actually enjoying the down time. No screaming kids, no overbearing mother telling me how I'm ruining my life. It's given me time to reflect. I realize it probably wasn't the best idea for me to show up at the courthouse like that. And I do feel bad about biting that woman's cheek. I saw a pretty face and I snapped. They told me I threatened to "suck her soul through her eye sockets," but honestly, I don't remember much. After the taste of blood hit my tongue, it was all a blur.

Have you ever tasted human flesh? I can see how people could get used to it. You know, if there was nothing else.

Anyway, I hope the trial is going well. I'm on what they call "psychiatric hold," and they don't let me watch the news or read the paper. I'm not even supposed to be writing you, so I don't know if you'll get this. But if by some chance you do, I want you to know I'm sorry for embarrassing you. The last thing I want is to hurt your chances of being exonerated.

In other news, Momma called and told me the state put Bobby and Derrik into foster care. (Sorry, guys! Mommy still loves you!) I know we never really talked about kids, but it's probably for the best. I need to concentrate on getting better. Then I can concentrate on us. The kids were just a distraction. Despite the bars in front of me, I feel free for the first time in my life. And I owe it all to you.

Love always,
Ginny

TWICE AMPUTATED FOOT

The first time my father had his foot amputated the surgery didn't take.

We're not talking a case of phantom limb, here. The morning after they severed the offending appendage, it reappeared. Just like that. Dad got up and walked around the hospital like nothing had happened.

It was the right foot, in case you were wondering.

"At least I didn't amputate the *wrong* foot," the surgeon said. He elbowed me in the ribs, winked at my brothers.

Ugh. If it looks like a duck and walks like a duck, it's probably a quack.

"How the hell is this even possible?" I said.

"Technically, it isn't." The surgeon tapped Dad's big toe with a pen. "We incinerated these little piggies hours ago. This, my friends, is a miracle."

Glares. In triplicate.

"Careful how you throw that word around," I told him. "Supernatural intervention is going to put you out of business."

At least my brothers and I were free to fly back to our respective lives. Not that we planned on hanging around either way. We had hired a Panamanian woman named Edna to take care of Dad. She didn't have any references, but she had hands bleached from cleaning and smelled like a home cooked meal. Of course, she didn't take the reappearance of the foot too well. She had already moved into *chez divorcee*, and dismissing her proved awkward.

"I come all this way from Panama," she said. It took a limo ride and a first class plane ticket to get rid of her. When we called six months later to tell her Dad was having the foot amputated again, she unleashed a torrent of irate Spanish and hung up.

Dad was adamant he hadn't been doing anything he wasn't supposed to when he broke his ankle the first time. He swore he hadn't been off the wagon.

"Were you dangling your foot over the edge? Did you get it caught in one of the wheels?" All I got for my humor was a grunt.

The surgeon said it was possible stepping out of bed caused the trimalleolar fracture. "Your father's in his sixties, after all."

I remained skeptical. You don't break your ankle in three places putting on your slippers.

The second time he hadn't been off the wagon, either. He had ridden it off a goddamn cliff, hollering the whole way down. At first the surgeon refused to perform the operation again. Said something about my father not respecting 'the finality of the procedure.' But once necrosis set in, Hippocrates would not be ignored.

This time the foot stayed amputated. After a week, Edna agreed to move back in, but only under the condition we sign her to a year contract. By the second month she no longer had to wait on Dad 'hand and footless' (another of the surgeon's jokes). They settled into the routine of a couple who would rather coexist in mutual indifference than admit defeat. A week before Edna's contract expired, my father made a surprise announcement.

"We're getting married."

"Who's we?"

"Edna and I."

"The housekeeper?"

"Watch it, boy. She's your mother now."

The wedding was an intimate affair. The ceremony took place in the living room, performed by a local minister. Edna's vast collection of Hummels served as witness.

Two weeks later, Edna moved her father in with them. The man was blind in one eye and borderline deaf. My brothers and I were against it, but Dad took to Diego right away. They'd sit in the living room with the TV on mute, never saying a word. It filled a family-sized hole in Dad's life.

"Better them than us," my middle brother said.

Another upshot of the union—it curtailed Dad's drinking. During his initial immobility he had to rely on Edna for his liquid fix. She would dole out just enough to keep him docile. But even after he could walk again, he rarely left the house, let alone his La-Z-Boy. His days of binge drinking came to an end.

Diego, on the other hand, couldn't drink due to poor liver function. Dad would let him smell his beer, which seemed to satisfy the man. I swear, sometimes it would give him a contact high.

We visited the following Thanksgiving, my youngest brother and I. My middle brother refused. He had declared a moratorium on interaction with our father. He only made exceptions for life or death situations. Like the dozen or so times our father drank himself into a coma. As far as the visiting patterns of neglectful children go, that put my brother way ahead of the game. To his face, we told him he was selfish. In reality, we envied his lack of empathy.

The surgeon took my brother's place at the dinner table. "I don't usually make house calls," he said, "but I worry when your father goes too long without injuring himself."

Dad did have quite the track record. Fractured ocular cavity due to a plumbing mishap, broken rib from coughing too hard, hand laceration from a drinking glass that had submicroscopic structural flaws—you name it, he claimed it happened to him.

Despite the interloper, everyone enjoyed the meal. Edna prepared what she referred to as a traditional Panamanian

Thanksgiving dinner. It consisted of *sancocho*, *arroz con guandu*, and something that tasted like fried fat. For dessert we had *hojaldras*, which turned out to be her word for Krispy Kreme donuts.

"Do they even celebrate Thanksgiving in Panama?" my youngest brother asked.

After dinner, we all watched football in the living room with the sound off. Even the surgeon, whose first name we learned was Robert. Diego spoke all of three English words, one of which was 'goal.' He'd say it every time a player scored a touchdown.

"Goal?" He said it as a question. Dad would nod in agreement, sip his ration of beer. Edna knitted in the corner. She smiled to herself, a de facto matriarch proud of the family she had cobbled together.

My real mother was over 1100 miles away, enjoying dinner with her own Frankenstein's Monster of a family. My parents had separated sooner than some couples, but later than most, and she found herself remarried to the owner of a high-end shoe store. The relationship came prepackaged with two adult daughters. My stepdad had an entire garage filled with single shoe samples, all for the right foot.

"Never for the *wrong* foot," he would say. My mother laughed every time. My middle brother would scowl. He hated living with Mom and her husband, but ever since he injured his back and went on disability he had no other viable option. So while I enjoyed *chicharrones* with Edna, Diego, and Robert, he slept through Thanksgiving, skulked upstairs to scavenge leftovers, and returned to his basement lair to sleep on a bed of Netflix and prescription pills.

"You know why you don't get along with Dad?" I told him one time. "Because you guys are too much alike. And not in a good way." He didn't appreciate that and declared a moratorium on speaking about our father.

Dear old Dad, who that Thanksgiving watched television with Diego while Robert made love to Edna in the other room. "Con permiso," he had told the surgeon. No one would be able to say he didn't provide for his wife, even if it was through a third party.

My youngest brother and I were already back at the motel, thank Christ. Poor Diego couldn't hear what was going on, but he knew. He gave my father a begrudging nod, the kind a man gives to acknowledge another man's sacrifice.

My father grimaced, struggled out of his recliner to the sound of muted grunting. He picked up the phone and dialed a number from muscle memory. The signal shot across hundreds of miles of telephone wire, routing through various switchboards and exchanges. In his mind it traveled a straight line, the shortest distance between the recipient and himself.

The phone on the other end lived under a pile of blankets in my mother's closet. It was an old line, but she couldn't bring herself to disconnect it. The sound of the ringing soothed my father. Plus, if she picked up, it wouldn't be him. It would be someone calling to tell her he was dead.

"Don't be so morbid," I would tell her. "After everything we've been through, his death will be more of a relief than anything." For a man who should have been dead five times over, or at the very least brain damaged, whose liver and kidneys would confound doctors for years to come, who walked away from numerous car crashes without a scratch— Dad would go quietly in his sleep.

Which is exactly what he did.

The last conversation I had with my father, he told me about a dream he'd had. He tended to ramble, and talking to him could be a real chore, but on this occasion he was particularly focused. In the dream, we were all gathered at his place for Christmas dinner: me, my brothers, Edna, Diego, Robert, my mother, and her husband. We ate in complete silence. It wasn't an awkward silence, we just didn't have anything to say. When the meal was over, we took turns telling each other the story of our lives. Like we had all just met for the first time. There were no tears or finger pointing. It was all about cause and effect, how we got from point A to point B. In a straight line or otherwise.

Then it was my father's turn. He tried to speak, but no one could see or hear him. He was a ghost.

"I wasn't sad, though," he said. "I was glad I got to listen to everyone's stories."

"Do you remember any of them?"

"No." He exhaled into the receiver. "That wasn't the point."

I nodded, even though he couldn't see me. After that, he chased a rabbit down a hole. I cut him off and made tentative plans to call again the following week. I never did. Three weeks later he was dead.

After the funeral we all gathered at his place, just like in his dream. An odd feeling of *déjà vu* permeated the room. Edna busied herself doing what she did best: taking care of people.

"She doesn't seem too upset," my youngest brother said.

"I don't think she expects this death to stick."

"It better."

The rest of the family did what they could to pass the time. Robert and my mother's husband engaged in a quiet conversation about feet. My ever attentive mother listened in. My middle brother watched television with Diego and the Hummels.

My foot tapped erratic, like a telegraph machine. *What hath God wrought?* I got the sudden urge to stand and get everyone's attention, so I could tell them my father's story. The one he never got to tell in his dream. But you know what? I couldn't. Because I didn't know it. I had never cared to. It had always interfered with my own story, like an unnecessary subplot.

But someone needed to say something. An exchange of information needed to take place. So I did the next best thing. I turned to my youngest brother and, with his help, began to piece together the details of our father's life. We started with his foot and worked our way backwards.

THE BLACK HOLE

As soon as Max crossed the event horizon, time began to slow.

From the outside there didn't appear to be anything particularly interesting about the place. No signage to identify it. Just a blank storefront with blacked-out windows, and, if you got close enough, *Abandon hope, all ye that enter here* carved into the door.

The establishment didn't need to advertise to survive. It catered to a specific clientele who were inexplicably drawn in by its gravitational pull. Max was one of them. He fit the image of the romanticized barfly, only ten years past his prime, face sunken and sallow. He had his father's disease in him, and had grown tired of fighting it.

On the other side of that door, blood would thin and light would bend as the present stretched beyond the infinite. The Doppler effect rendered patrons forever young, until they entered the singularity and blinked out of existence. Until then, they drank.

Max sat with his back to the door, as if to ignore it, as if he could leave if he wanted. He raised his glass to eye-level and studied the meniscus of the clear liquid. As time slowed inside the bar it moved faster on the outside world. Molly would be turning six soon. He'd miss her birthday, but she'd get over it. Until the following year when it happened again, that is. He tried not to picture her big brown eyes brimming with tears, that adorable little pout. Anne would be there for her and would make him the bad guy — which he was — and that would help them through the hurt.

"How's the little one?" the bartender asked, as if on cue. He looked like a regular who had wandered onto the wrong side of the bar and put on an apron.

"Not so little anymore. She's in junior high now."

"You don't say? Seems like just yesterday she turned six years old. "

"She's co-captain of the pep squad, whatever that is."

"Isn't that something? They sure grow up fast, don't they?"

"Faster every day. In fact, she's about to graduate high school. Top of her class. She's going to the prom with what's-his-name? The Baker kid."

"Billy?"

"No, the younger one. Brett. Good kid. Knows how to keep his hands to himself."

Nods and sighs segued into lapsed conversation. All their exchanges went like this. Recycled pleasantries to pass the time.

"Molly's leaving for Amherst next week."

"You don't say? Gosh, they grow up fast."

"Faster every day. You should see her. Looks just like her mother."

The first few years had been hard, but Molly moved on with her life. The mental image she had of her father remained unchanged from the time she turned six, because she hadn't seen him since. He had exited her life and become unstuck in time.

"How *are* things with the ex?" the bartender asked Max.

"She's doing well. Had a cancer scare, but everything's okay now."

"That's good to hear. Get you another?"

"Wife? No thanks. One was enough."

The bartender smiled and wagged his finger, as if to say

why yooooou... Max downed the last of his drink and slid the glass forward a couple inches.

"She's getting married again. Can you believe it?"

"Jeez. Time sure does move fast, doesn't it?"

"Not in here it doesn't." More nods and sighs.

Molly graduated Amherst *cum laude* with an interdisciplinary degree in religion, astronomy and women's studies, but declined to accept her diploma during the commencement ceremony. Instead, she stood at the back of the auditorium in silent protest over not being conferred the distinction of *summa cum laude*. This occurred shortly after her mother's illness, and even though she managed to keep her grades up, she missed a lot of days and they penalized her for not filing an official leave of absence.

"Tyrannical bureaucratic bullshit. Said it right to the Dean's face," Max told the bartender.

"Ha! That kid's a firecracker."

"She sure is. Did I tell you she's getting married?"

"No kidding?"

"Nice guy. I think he's a veterinary assistant or something. Works with animals."

"Girls love a guy who loves animals. Another drink?"

Molly and Eric married in a small civil ceremony presided over by a Justice of the Peace. Eric's brother filled the role of best man. Molly's mom stood in as Maid of Honor. Immediately afterwards, the newlyweds drove up to the Poconos for their honeymoon.

Molly had been obsessed with Mount Airy Lodge since childhood. To her, the word *honeymoon* was synonymous with *champagne glass jacuzzi*. Developers tore the original resort down in the aughts, but a casino had been built in its place. A few of the boarded up old buildings still existed out in the woods—mostly employee housing—and the happy couple went exploring, ouija board in tow. They attempted to contact the spirit of original owner Emil Wagner, who had committed suicide after the resort shut down.

"I blame those damn commercials," Max told the

bartender. "She always sang that stupid theme song. *All you have to bring, is your love of everything...*"

"*Beautiful Mount Airy Loooooooodge!*" They sang the last part together.

"She used to think 'beautiful' was part of the resort's name," Max said.

Nods and sighs. The spaces between these conversations grew. The bar had no clock, so Max couldn't gauge the time.

Molly and Eric waited until Eric opened his own veterinary practice to have their first child. They named the little girl Button, as in *cute as a...* Molly's mom railed against it at first.

"Other kids will make fun of her!" she said. But as soon as she held her granddaughter that first time, no other name would do.

"Can you believe I'm a grandfather?" Max said.

The bartender poured them both a shot. "I'll drink to that. This one's on me."

Two years later Anne's cancer returned. She held on for a good six years before she passed. But those years took a toll on Molly and Eric. Towards the end Anne moved in with them, and Molly took care of her full time. After the funeral Molly withdrew, and she and Eric drifted apart. They stayed together for their daughter, but divorced after she graduated high school.

"I remember when Molly graduated high school," Max said to the bartender. "Seems like only yesterday. Now I've got a granddaughter going to college."

"Time sure does move fast on the outside, don't it?"

"Sure does."

"Well, if it's any consolation, you don't look old enough to be a grandfather. You haven't aged a day since you walked through that door."

Max looked over his shoulder and squinted at the entrance. The sliver of light slipping underneath flared due to increased blueshift. He turned back to the bartender, spots dotting his vision. "Give me another," he said to the biggest one.

It took a while, but Molly and Eric became friends after the divorce. She even took a job as a receptionist at the clinic. When Button came home from school for the holidays they would all get together for dinner.

"I go by 'Bee' now," she told her parents on one such occasion. "Also, I think I'm in love with a girl." Eric choked on his food. Molly kicked him under the table.

"That's wonderful, dear," Molly said.

Bee brought Amanda home to meet her parents that Christmas. The two behaved like long lost sisters. After they graduated they moved to a coffee farm in Hawaii. They adopted two girls of their own. Hannah and Lily.

They didn't get to visit often, so Molly spent a lot of time at home by herself. Despite a genetic predisposition to addiction she had never had a problem with drinking. Only now did she start to feel the pull. She pulled back by going to Al-Anon meetings.

"Good people," Max told the bartender. "Their hearts're in the right place."

"Bad for business," the bartender said.

At Al-Anon they encouraged Molly to confront the place where she lost her father. That's how she found herself standing in front of the boarded up facade of what used to be The Black Hole. She traced the Dante quote with her fingertips. The elements had smoothed the splintered edges of the words. She reached for the doorknob.

On the inside, Max approached the edge of the singularity. He turned to look towards the entrance again. The light on the outside shined through the door, rendering it transparent. He could see his daughter, now an old woman, standing on the other side.

She could see him as well. The man who left her when she was six, just as she remembered him. Although his image stood frozen in time, Molly swore he looked at her. Sadness welled in his eyes.

Max's image began to flicker. Molly watched as it became more erratic. She watched until it winked out of existence, as Max crossed the threshold of the singularity.

After he disappeared, the light faded and the door became solid once again.

An infinite speed up occurred, and Max saw the history of the universe unfold in an instant. Not just the death of his adult daughter, who walked back home and cried herself to sleep that night. Not just the death of his granddaughter and her grandchildren—the death of humanity. He witnessed generations, eons, apocalypse. The rebirth of life as evolution started from scratch, as it had done so many times before, and the death of that life as well. Innumerable cycles. He witnessed the beginning and end of life on other planets, the birth and death of stars, the death of entire galaxies. Radiation bombarded Max as the universe ended and the light blueshifted into infinity. Infinity then nothing, as he fell into the wormhole.

Then from within the nothing, there appeared a million tiny dots, like pinpricks in black paper. Atoms, maybe. Or stars. Growing larger. He focused on one. It was a door. The door of The Black Hole, transparent and glowing. On the other side he could see the silhouette of six-year-old Molly, reaching for the handle. That never happened, did it? There were a million other Molly's at a million other doors, reaching for a million handles. Some of them opened the door and went in. Some of them didn't. They lived a million other lives, each of them unique. Max longed to know each and every one of them, escape the gravity of the bar and be part of their lives. But it was too late. Once you crossed the event horizon, you could never escape. You could only watch.

He chose to watch the six-year-old girl he left behind, her hand hovering above the handle. If he had any breath left in his lungs, Max would have held it. Or better yet, if sound waves traveled fast enough to escape the singularity, he would have used that breath to yell. But they didn't, and he couldn't. Molly was an object set in motion, and unless an outside force prevented her, she would turn the handle and walk through that door. Max prepared to have his heart broken for the very first time.

But something held her back. Molly returned her hand to her side without having touched the door. She walked home and cried herself to sleep, just as adult Molly had. Max watched it all. He existed at the center of both their universes and a million others. The singularity of infinite density that birthed their lives even as it destroyed them. A destruction that spanned all time, in the blink of an eye.

He smiled, and millions of doors coalesced into a giant ball of light.

HOMUNCULOID

A Brief Overview of the Controversial Mid-21st Century
Computer Game

*Welcome back to BLASTERS FROM THE PAST, a monthly
column dedicated to exploring the world of classic videogames. From
the Cathode Ray Amusement Devices of the mid 20th Century to
the next-gen super-consoles and beyond, we are dedicated to the
preservation of electronic gaming history.*

*In this installment, we take a look at one of the last great
MMORPGs of the 21st Century—the controversial hit,
HOMUNCULOID, produced by Mandrake Studios.*

Type of Game:
MMORPG, or Massively Multiplayer Online Role Playing
Game. A style popularized in the late 20th Century, and a
direct precursor to the current Universal Gaming Platform
in which all games exist in a single, interactive universe
stored on Cumulus. HOMUNCULOID has been described
as a cross between *The Sims*, *Second Life*, and *Grand Theft
Auto* with an RPG-style attribute system. The game represents a logical progression from those classics (each of which
has been explored in previous columns), as it reimagines the

life simulation genre by raising the stakes and incorporating
a more meaningful form of social commentary.

Objective:
To be born an Entity of Means and Privilege, or EMP.

Character:
You are Homunculoid, formed of spit and clay, gestated in a
fermented horse womb by Paracelus, The Alchemist,
birthed into one of two Statuspheres within The Known
World.

Setup:
A third person sandboxer set in the early 21st Century,
HOMUNCULOID is a true rarity: a game where your fate
(i.e.: completion of the Objective) is determined by chance,
as opposed to player proficiency. In addition, completion of
the Objective (or failure to do so) occurs at the beginning of
the gameplay session, rather than the end. Despite this, the
player is required to finish out the Story Mode, making
superfluous decisions that may affect their "life," but have
no effect on the predetermined outcome of the game.

Gameplay:
At the onset of gameplay, a random Ethnic Aesthetic is
assigned, determining your Social Status. If the Objective of
the game has been achieved, an existence of varying degrees
of frivolity is awarded. As an EMP, the player has limited
Interaction Restrictions and a low Rate of Consequence.
They are free to pursue, explore, and enjoy. It is possible, if
one achieves the Objective, to finish out the Story Mode
focusing on the betterment of those who didn't (known as
Differently Fortunates), although this is considered a futile
endeavor within the social structure of the game. It does,
however, boost the EMP's Perceived Self Worth.

If the Objective is not achieved, continuation of the
playthrough, though mandatory, is a moot exercise. A

Differently Fortunate has many more Interaction Restrictions and a much higher Rate of Consequence, resulting in a greater Endangerment Level (determined by Gender and Gentry, amongst other metrics) and a shorter Lifespan.

Average completion time depends on the Assigned Ethnic Aesthetic and Social Ranking of your character. A successful EMP can "live" between 700 to 1000 game hours, but a DF's Lifespan is inversely proportional to their Endangerment Level. Movement between Economic Strata is possible, but Ethnic Aesthetics cannot be modified. Gender can be reassigned, but this does not necessarily result in improved ranking.

Environment:
Setting is a mixture of pre-industrial and post-apocalyptic, with both rural and metropolitan locales, existing under a conservative political entity in a borderline dystopia. Interaction with the Governing Hierarchy varies wildly based on Ethnic Aesthetic and a character's Provocation Ethic. The better your standing with the Governing Hierarchy, the less restrictions will be placed on your Allowable Radius of Migration.

Visually, the game design holds up remarkably well, even by the standards of today's holographics. The photorealistic modeling and lifelike character animation make for a thoroughly immersive storytelling experience.

Walkthrough:
As a Differently Fortunate
Since winning or losing is a completely randomized event, there is little purpose in offering a traditional walkthrough explaining how to complete the game's Objective. In the past, numerous intranetwork communities existed for different character Aesthetics. These communities acted as a type of surrogate family to help guide DFs through the Story Mode. Although every Story Mode experience is

unique, there are certain strategies that apply to most DF playthroughs:

— You can't choose your Aesthetic, but the initial moments after a DF emerges from the Amniosis (literally: horse wine) are crucial. You are born fully formed, but diminutive. Seek a safe environment within which to increase your Mass of Form. This growth period is considered by many players to be a highlight of the game. Less restrictions are imposed on gameplay, thus permitting a level of freedom rarely later attained in the character's Lifespan.

— Directly following this period, you may choose to pursue Educational Enhancement, although the Resources and Opportunities available to you will be scant. These are generally reserved for EMPs with very few Advancement Impediments (due to the accumulation of Grandfather Points, which can be gifted from EMP to EMP). No such point system exists for Differently Fortunates. Still, pursuit of Educational Enhancement is a worthwhile endeavor.

— Instead of/in addition to Educational Enhancement, you may choose to participate in Workforce! The earlier you enter the so-called Occupation Stream, the less likely you will be branded as Non-Contributing. You will also begin accruing Barter Tokens, which are necessary for survival after the gestation period.

Pro-tip: While amassing Barter Tokens can be beneficial, remember the immortal words of one of the games more popular celebrity characters: mo' Barter Tokens, mo' Problematic Interactions.

— Align yourself with a philanthropic EMP early on. It can be demeaning, but being a Philanthropet has its advantages.

— You can also choose to align yourself with other Differently Fortunates, and organize a Mutual Support Network, but you run the risk of being branded as Militant by the Governing Hierarchy if that Network grows too large.

— Cultural Appropriation is considered a powerful camouflage technique. Acquiring the appropriate culture-mods may render you less intimidating to EMPs, but be aware, Cultural Appropriation is a two-way street.

— A Declared Spiritual Affiliation has its social advantages. However, remember: even though The Alchemist created you, he will never, ever intervene on your behalf.

As an EMP

If you win the Genetic Lottery (Alchemist be praised, but not depended upon, as the game intones), The Known World is your oyster. You can choose to become a Productive Member of Society, or you can live a Consequence Free Lifestyle. These are a few of the gameplay options with which to celebrate your lack of Empathy. Players can:

— Start a Sex Cult. Everything is legal when you have Spiritual Exemption, and limited startup capital is required. Once an in-game Church gets going, it practically pays for itself. (Note: Spiritual Exemption does not extend to Same Sex Sex Cults.)

— Destroy an Economic Infrastructure. In HOMUNCULOID, building something up isn't half as much fun as tearing it down. And if you run out of Barter Tokens, the Governmental Hierarchy will not hesitate to institute a Waterbucket Mandate.

— Get away with murder. Literally.

—Achieve Celebristatus by entering the Wide World of Professional Politics, which is part of the Entertainment Arm of the Governmental Hierarchy. A love of meaningless, high stakes competition is ingrained in the game's AI.

Pro Tip: The whole enterprise is an obvious farce, like
Professional Wrestling, but that doesn't mean it can't be
used to your advantage.

— You can also start a Blog.

Custom Skin Modding:
Although an Assigned Ethnic Aesthetic cannot be changed,
there are Custom Skin Mods that allow EMPs to alter their
general appearance. One of the more popular Mods is the
Somatosensory Mod, which allows the EMP to resize its
body parts according to physical sensitivity, typically
resulting in comically proportioned limbs and genitals. As
an EMP, you are permitted to wield said genitals with
impunity. This Mod can be unlocked by pursuing a Workforce! Occupation Placement in the Neurotosciences.

Replication:
Both EMPs and Differently Fortunates are capable of Replication, or creating Homunculoids of their very own.
However, these are not created in the same manner The
Alchemist created you. Homunculoidal Reproduction is
achieved via the expulsion of mini-Homunculoids (also
called "Animalcules") present in the spermatozoa. These are
then deposited in the Gestation Bank of a (preferably, but
not necessarily) Willing Participant, where they must stay
until they become large enough to survive Post Womb. If a
Participant is not Willing to bring your progeny to Term,
you can enlist the Governmental Hierarchy to modify their
Agreements to the Term.

Interesting side note: Since every male Homunculoid is
equipped with a flesh satchel full of Animalcules, each with
their own satchel full of even smaller Animalcules, we are
presented with a Paradox of Infinite Reducibility, *ad
absurdum*. Basically, it's testicles all the way down.

Replication is not recommended for the inexperienced

gamer playing as a Differently Fortunate. Despite the potential raising of your Fulfillment Index, it is a considerable drain on time and resources better spent on your own survival.

Consensus:

Even if you do not complete the game's Objective, Story Mode is still a rewarding, albeit challenging, endeavor. Although controversial at the time of its release, HOMUNCULOID has since developed a strong following among retro-gamers and is now considered a classic of the era, despite what is viewed as a flaw in its goal structure.

In fact, most gamers consider a playthrough as a Differently Fortunate to be the preferred mode of gameplay. The limitations and restrictions placed on the DF are largely responsible for the game's enduring popularity, since many of the problems of the time period have been all but eradicated by modern society. There is an element of cultural tourism at play in HOMUNCULOID, seeing as how the hardships it depicts are largely relics of a thankfully bygone era rife with unfortunate economic and political absurdities.

This would no doubt come as a surprise to the game's developers at Mandrake Studios, who, despite their intentions with the creative direction of HOMUNCULOID, managed to produce a hit game with lasting social impact. An impact that has outlasted their own company, which went bankrupt shortly after the game's release.

MAISON D'OEUFS

The limo glided past the entrance, an apex predator made of reinforced steel. Martha peered over the top of her Dolce and Gabbana sunglasses, through tinted windows, at the crowd gathered out front.

"Shit," the driver said. "Should I go around back?"

"That won't be necessary."

The driver pulled to the curb. His reflection studied Martha from the rearview.

"You sure? Those assholes can get pretty nasty."

"Without those assholes, this place wouldn't exist."

The driver gave a blank stare as the woman adjusted her glasses. "I don't follow."

Martha pulled out a compact and inspected her face. Middle age stared back at her. "It's symbiotic. Activism rides the coattails of the trends, and vice versa." She dusted a cosmetic sponge and attempted to smooth out the wrinkles in her skin.

The driver nodded, then stopped. "I still don't follow."

"Then maybe you should consider leading?" Martha snapped the compact shut and motioned toward the passenger side door. It took a moment for the hint to register.

"Right. Sorry."

The driver exited the vehicle and circled around to open Martha's door. She extended a toned leg. The click of stiletto heel on sidewalk set the protestors in motion. Head down, she followed the driver as the crowd converged on her with their signs. She flashed back to that day at the clinic, all those years ago. The accusations were the same. *Monster. Murderer.*

At least this time she didn't have to brave it alone. The driver parted the angry mob and led her safely to the door. She looked back at the protestors and sneered. All this fuss over something so small.

The door swung shut behind her, muting the rabble. A woman in a white pantsuit stood before her.

"Good evening. May I take your coat?"

Martha shrugged out of her leather jacket, which she had worn despite the summer heat. The—receptionist? Hostess?—folded it over her arm.

"Right this way, please."

She led Martha down a hallway into a small waiting area. Leather chairs, glass table, expensive art books. A framed photo of a single orchid hung on the main wall. A woman about Martha's age, years not hidden as well, sat in the corner, dwarfed by a book on fashion photography.

"If you'd have a seat, please." Martha's escort flashed a smile and disappeared, the glint of her teeth lingering like a ghost.

The other woman looked up as Martha sat, gave a tentative nod. Underneath her finery existed an air of desperation. Makeup caked folds of loose skin. Martha resented being in the same room as her.

"Is this your first time?" the woman said from behind the book, a contorted waif on the cover.

"Yes." Martha gritted her teeth.

"I've been here four, five times now. It does wonders." The woman stuck out her chin and waved a hand in the air to illustrate her point.

"I see."

The woman took the comment at face value. "I would

have pegged you for a repeat customer yourself, as good as you look."

Martha smiled and scanned the table for a book to use as a social buffer. She pushed aside a book on Modernist Cuisine, recoiled from a book of Lennart Nilsson's photography.

"Nervous?" the woman said.

"Not really." Martha's stomach fluttered.

"You know, it isn't nearly as bad as you'd expect."

It isn't nearly as good, if your face is the result. Martha hated waiting rooms, now more than ever. She tuned the woman out, flashed back to *that day*.

"We're too young for this," her high school boyfriend had told her. This was on the phone, the night before. Not at the clinic, when she needed reassurance she'd made the right choice. It was time that convinced her of that. So what her motives had been selfish?

The hostess reappeared in the doorway. The chatty woman hadn't stopped talking.

"Bending the ear again, Mrs. Wheeler?"

"Just making small talk. Is my table ready?"

"It is."

Mrs. Wheeler eased herself from under the weight of the book. She patted Martha's hand on her way out.

"Trust me, dear. It's worth it."

———

The hostess led Martha through a pair of double doors, seated her in a stiff, high-backed chair at the center of a white room. A cold light glinted off the utensils on the table before her. They resembled surgical instruments. She reached out and picked up a long, thin spoon. Felt its weight. She had a flash of it scraping around inside her and dropped it with a gasp.

"I'll get that, ma'am." The hostess knelt to retrieve the utensil. A server, also in white, simultaneously replaced it with a new one.

"Thank you," Martha said. It came out soft. She took a sip of water, hadn't realized how dry her throat was.

"Would you like to see today's selections?"

The server presented her with a large, leather menu. It unfolded into three sections, each with a picture of a young woman in nude colored panties standing against a white backdrop. Two brunettes and one blonde. All three suggested a younger version of Martha.

"They've all been..."

"Yes, Ma'am. *In vitro*, of course."

"Right." She tapped a fingernail on the one to the left.

"Very good, ma'am." The server whisked the menu away.

At the same time, impossibly soon, another server appeared and laid a domed, silver tray before her. She saw her distorted reflection in the metal and held her breath.

The server whipped off the cover with a flourish to reveal a small, crystal dish. It contained a minuscule helping of what appeared to be globules of yellow jelly, quivering atop a single leaf of lettuce.

Martha exhaled.

"That's it?"

"Would madame like something different?"

"No, this will be fine. Thank you."

The server receded into the shadows. Martha picked up her utensil. The entire portion amounted to one spoonful. She didn't see the big deal. They didn't even look like eggs.

She raised the spoon to her mouth. *Maybe I should look up that old boyfriend*, she thought.

MUMMER'S PARADE

Triboulet was known throughout the realm for having the King's ear. He wore it around his neck on a silver chain. Despite a coating of embalmer's wax it gave off the faint whiff of rot, which he did not find unpleasant. The sickly sweet smell served to reassure him his prized possession rested safe against his chest.

When dark things needed doing he would press his wet lips against the cartilage and whisper. The words he entrusted to the severed lobe were privy only to his mummers—animals with human faces that carried out his commands. They existed in the cold and shadows of the once vibrant throne room.

Triboulet groaned as he massaged his misshapen head. The pressure had worsened, and the protests of the rabble outside the keep didn't help. Both problems would have to be dealt with soon. He had barely slept in a fortnight.

He tried to imagine how his predecessor would have handled the situation. The King had always heeded Triboulet's counsel, even before Triboulet relieved him of his ear. In fact, Triboulet had grown to become one of the King's most trusted advisors. But then the fluid on his brain debilitated his speech to the point where it lost all coherence. As Triboulet did not know how to read or write, communication between the two became all but impossible. The mummers started to appear shortly thereafter.

Their hijinks proved a welcome distraction from the mundanity of daily existence. They deciphered Triboulet's garbled speech with ease, and when hard decisions needed making they'd tell him what to do, relieving him of the burden of conscience.

Triboulet looked down at his scarlet tunic and wiped at a spot of drool. He had never wanted to be a performer. He wasn't a particularly good one. Aside from his short stature and grotesque appearance, he offered little in the way of amusement. But no one had given him a choice in the matter.

His parents had been dirt farmers, peasants lacking the means to support a child suffering an affliction such as his. He'd almost killed his mother during childbirth and hadn't been expected to live out his first year. So they took it as good fortune when a caravan of revelers draped in animal skin marched out of the snow, seeking shelter for the evening. Their leader, the fox, took pity on Triboulet, and offered a purse of gold in exchange for the boy.

"The child will be well cared for," it said.

Triboulet's parents had never seen so much money. It didn't take them long to make a decision. *It is for his own good,* they told themselves, even before the fox said the same.

Triboulet still remembered the face that had peered out from beneath the pelt as his father sealed the deal with a handshake. It belonged to the man he had betrayed, the man upon whose throne he currently sat.

He felt a pang of remorse, and decided to counteract it with drink. He whispered into the King's ear. The bear rolled out on its ball, balancing a flagon atop a tray. The creature watched from behind its human mask as Triboulet gulped down the wine. The liquid hit his belly and sent warm tendrils spreading throughout his body. It soothed the pounding in his head.

Triboulet never blamed his parents for sending him away.

Even though he hated being gawked at like a sideshow freak, he loved the freedom of travel, sleeping under the stars with the rest of the actors. It was the only time he truly felt happy. He even learned to enjoy the ritual of performance, his rote delivery of punchlines developing a certain panache. But all that changed when the troupe returned to the citadel, and the then-Prince had to get down to the business of ruling.

For you see, a career as a traveling actor was never in the cards for the young Prince. He had been granted a reprieve from duty to sow his wild oats, as it were, in exchange for the assurance he would dedicate himself to the interests of the royal family upon his return. This included conceding to an arranged marriage and an abandonment of his dreams of the stage.

It wasn't a bad life. His bride to be was a pleasant enough girl he would grow to love, a girl Triboulet would grow to covet. Her image dominated his lustful thoughts during his darkest hours.

The transition period was a short one, as the King had fallen ill during his son's wanderings. Once the Prince became the new King, he did his best to honor the promise he made to Triboulet's parents, but the Council would only permit the imp to attend court garbed in a fool's motley. He lived in comfort, but the cruelty of men stifled his heart. They would snicker behind his back, mocking his distended skull and taut skin. He retaliated by filling the King's ear with poisonous words.

Many men lost their heads as a result. First on the chopping block was the King's personal physician. The man had been charged with monitoring Triboulet's physical well being, but had never successfully improved his patient's condition, no matter how many bitter concoctions he forced him to drink.

Initially the King interpreted the request as a joke. Triboulet had refused to cooperate with the physician one day, having had his fill of experimental potions. He led the man on a wild chase around the examination room, generally making a nuisance of himself. The physician, his patience at an end, threatened to vivisect Triboulet to determine the cause of his malady. Triboulet did not find this amusing. He reported the offense to the King, who laughed it off.

"Do not worry," the King said. "If the man decides to cut you into pieces, I'll have him relieved of his head before a quarter hour has passed," to which Triboulet replied, "Would it not be possible to relieve him of his head a quarter hour before?" The King laughed even harder, stopping only when he saw the look in Triboulet's eyes.

"You can't be serious," the King said. But Triboulet was adamant.

He became addicted to the influence he wielded. The thrill of holding his perceived enemies' lives in his hand. The look of fear in people's eyes when they saw him lean towards the King. Certain factions considered him the most powerful man in all the kingdom. Alas, his reign ended prematurely.

When he could no longer speak due to his illness and the King stopped seeking his advice, Triboulet took it as a betrayal. He summoned his mummers and had the King deposed. To this day, the scribes remain unable to explain how he managed such a coup. Those who objected were silenced with the knife.

Amongst the objectors was the King's own son. He and Triboulet had been raised as brothers, and out of respect for that bond Triboulet offered to let the Prince choose the manner of his own death. In a final attempt to appeal to Triboulet's waning humanity, the Prince had requested to be sentenced to die of old age, a reference to a joke from Triboulet's days of performing with the King's troupe. It achieved the opposite of the desired effect, however, sending Triboulet into a rage, resulting in a more immediate form of execution for the Prince.

Then there was the matter of the King's wife, the object of Triboulet's pathetic affection. The deposition of her husband and execution of her son did little to ingratiate

Triboulet to her romantically. He found it necessary to take nefarious actions.

On more than one occasion the King's alchemist had claimed he regularly transformed himself into a newt, so that he might sneak up on chambermaids in the bath, unobserved, and witness the pampering of their soft flesh, all hot and pink from the steam. He offered to aid Triboulet in his own titillating subterfuge.

But the noxious potion the alchemist poured down Triboulet's throat only resulted in making him *think* himself a newt, and the Queen noticed him almost immediately, perched on her nightstand, naked and unblinking, chubby tongue flicking in and out at imaginary flies. He retreated from her quarters covered in the contents of her chamber pot.

There was no coming back from such humiliation. It pained Triboulet to waste such beauty, but he found it necessary to dispose of the Queen. It was either her or the alchemist, and despite his failings the alchemist had not yet outlasted his usefulness.

Triboulet raised his head as a cry went up from outside the keep. The crowd had grown in number. It wouldn't be long before the King's governors arrived with reinforcements. Most of the messenger birds had been shot down, but rats could go where men could not and trained surprisingly easy. Even now the filthy beasts might be burrowing their way to his enemies, informing them of his every move. Triboulet addressed the King's ear and dispatched his mummers to investigate.

"Nuut. Yuuu." he said to the bear. "Uughnutter." He threw the flagon to the floor, the clattering of the vessel echoing throughout the empty hall. The bear rolled over and scooped it up in one fluid motion, balance never faltering.

Triboulet didn't usually drink this much. Alcohol exacerbated his condition. He became maudlin, wondering if he might have been better off left to die on his parents' farm. He longed to go back to that moment in time, when they had traded him for a purse of gold, beg them to reconsider.

The alchemist insisted the feat was still possible. In addition to the power of transformation, he claimed mastery over time itself, achieved with the aid of Psilocybic spores. Unfortunately his temporal travels did not include his corporeal self, which he left unguarded and usually found soiled in its own filth upon returning. After the newt deba-cle, Triboulet was loath to trust the man again. Still...

The bear returned with the wine, which Triboulet downed in one gulp. His eyes teared and his vision blurred. The clash of steel rang outside the keep and his brain regis-tered the smell of smoke. It was only a matter of time. He slurred words into the severed ear like a lecherous drunk, teetering on the edge of consciousness. The badger appeared not a moment later, leading the trembling alchemist before him.

"Your Grace."

Triboulet lifted his head. Although the alcohol made it feel lighter, it also made it harder to support. He steadied it with his hand, lest his neck should snap under its weight.

The alchemist stood before him, proffering a steaming chalice. Triboulet beckoned and the man put the cup to his lips and helped him drink. More than half of it dribbled down his chin.

"Forgive me, your Grace." The alchemist wiped at Triboulet's tunic with his hand. Triboulet swatted him away.

"Let me get you some more. If a full dose is not imbibed—"

Triboulet promptly vomited all over himself and the alchemist.

The alchemist took a step back, fear hiding the disgust in his eyes. He watched as Triboulet's head lolled and eyes crossed. The imp reached for the ear around his neck but couldn't find it—the alchemist had brushed it aside while trying to clean his tunic. He looked down at his chest in order to locate the ear, but his head weighed too much, and the forward momentum brought him crashing off the throne and onto his face. His stubby arms paddled the air, as if he swam through his own vomit. His body twitched— once, twice— and then he lay still. The whole time the alchemist watched, not knowing what to do.

"Your Grace?"

No response. The alchemist scanned the empty hall. No mummers in sight. He took a tentative step backwards.

"Your Grace?"

The alchemist turned and ran.

"Your Grace?"

Triboulet looked up to find the badger standing before him. The alchemist was nowhere to be seen. Somehow Triboulet had gotten back onto the throne. Someone had cleaned the vomit as well, though there were remnants of it on his tunic.

"It is time," the badger said.

"Veddy. Gourrrd."

Triboulet crawled down from the throne, taking his empty flagon with him. He would have the bear refill it for the road. Purging his stomach had made him feel much better, although he couldn't be positive it had actually happened. He made a mental note to have the alchemist tortured to death either way.

The badger escorted the inebriated imp through a maze of dank corridors to the King's cell. The creature's torch cast a flickering light upon a heap of tattered robes within. Triboulet raked his flagon across the cell bars, prompting an exodus of rats. If any of them carried pleas for help, they would arrive too late.

The heap raised its head, revealing a festering wound where an ear should be.

"Hello, old friend." The swelling of infection prevented the King from smiling. "To what do I owe the honor?"

Triboulet said nothing as the pale man rose to meet him. His body trembled from the exertion, but at a good three feet taller than Triboulet he struck an imposing figure.

Triboulet brought the King's ear up to his lips and whispered.

"I am here to right a great wrong." The badger spoke for Triboulet, who fixed his eyes on the captive. He witnessed the tiniest ember of hope.

"But to do that, I'm afraid I'm going to need the rest."

The King's countenance fell as he realized what this meant.

Triboulet flipped up the hood of his tunic to reveal the fox head pelt, the one the King had worn all those years before. It barely concealed his deformity. He signaled for the badger to unlock the cell and drew a wavy-bladed *kris* from its sheath. Two more mummers appeared from the shadows —the deer and the jackrabbit—to hold the King down. He did not resist.

Upstairs, the rabble penetrated the keep's fortifications. The stomping of their boots shook dust from stone as they spread out and searched the castle. Triboulet smirked. They had arrived too late. He could already feel the time altering effects of the alchemist's potion. The noise from above helped block out the King's screams as Triboulet carved the skin from his face.

———

The parade of mummers marched single-file through the snow, appearing as if out of nowhere. Bears, wolves, badgers, deer—all led by the fox, all wearing their human faces. Their torches cast eerie shadows that danced alongside them, merry in their mischief.

As they approached the farmhouse the fox gave the signal to stop. The mummers complied but their shadows remained restless. The fox adjusted its human face before continuing to the door alone. It did not expect any resistance. The place looked barely capable of providing protection from the elements. The fox raised its hand and knocked.

A peasant woman answered, a young boy with a cephalic disorder clutching at her leg. The child looked up at the fox. The face of the King peered out from beneath its snout.

Although the child had never seen the face before, it possessed a familiarity. Still, something didn't feel right. Grey skin hung loose, jagged flaps sticking out at the sides. The eyes existed in shadowed hollows. A trickle of blood crept down the side of its neck.

The mouth beneath the King's face smiled at the boy as the fox slowly withdrew its *kris*. The boy tightened his grip on his mother's leg. Dreams of golden coins dotting the night sky faded from time's memory. The curtain drew closed as the actors prepared to take their final bows.

"Doonught. Buuurry. " Triboulet said to his younger self, spittle dribbling from the mask's paper thin lips. "Dis. Brill. Pfffecks."

The mummers turned their backs and disappeared into the snow as the fox raised its knife. They took their foot-prints and their shadows with them. They took the peasant woman and the farmhouse and the trees. All sound receded as if in a vacuum. Soon only the fox and the boy remained, Triboulet and his younger self, standing in a field of white.

The remnants of the alchemist's potion gurgled in Triboulet's stomach. The inside of the King's face grew humid with his breath. The boy shifted in and out of focus, waiting patiently for his fate to be decided, as if he already knew the outcome.

Triboulet blinked his eyes shut, slow. In certain animals, this was considered a sign of trust. It was also used to lull enemies into a false sense of security. The boy returned the gesture. Only one set of eyes would open again. And when they did, they would find themselves lying alone in a pool of their own blood, knife buried to the hilt in their throat. Thunder would shake the sky like applause, all of creation rising to its feet in a standing ovation.

THE END

THE HAND OF GOD

He could feel the hand of God, fingers wrapped tight around his throat.

Jack opened one eye. The preacher's hands hadn't moved. One palmed Jack's forehead while the other petitioned the sky. Two additional sets of hands held Jack's arms aloft.

Too many hands.

The preacher's mouth was a lipless mass of scarred flesh. It stretched and pulled thin in an attempted smile. The invisible hand of The Almighty tightened its grip.

Jack's vision blurred and dimmed. The warble of the organ became muffled. He could feel the congregation on the edge of his fading senses, but they made no move to help him.

He gasped, tried to call out to them, and then another hand was in his mouth. It grabbed ahold of his tongue. An alphabet of fire poured into his stomach.

He retched, vomited the letters back up in random order, spewing the Spirit's bile in a mellifluous stream of praise. And then he was falling backwards, in a slow motion arc towards the floor.

All those hands. Will any of them catch me?

Jack awoke with a start, heart kicking against his ribs.

Someone had been screaming in a foreign language. He spent several alert moments breathing in the dark before the panic subsided and it hit him. The voice had been his own.

He got up to get a glass of water. He rented a room from an elderly couple that attended his parents' church. He shared a kitchen with them, which meant meals came with a side of that old-time religion. On the plus side, the place was cheap and his night terrors didn't pose an issue for the hearing impaired couple. And at least he had his own bathroom—one of the few places he could hide from the omnipresent reach of The Lord.

He filled his glass and studied his reflection in the mirror. The skin around his throat flared angry and red.

———

"Sounds like demonic possession to me."

Esther had that look in her eye. The same one she got when she solved an especially difficult crossword clue. She pushed back a mess of dark hair as if she wanted Jack to see it, see that she had him figured out.

"Stands to reason you can be possessed by God," she said. "Same as the devil."

"You know I don't believe in that shit."

"The greatest trick the devil ever pulled was convincing mankind he didn't exist."

"Yeah, I saw that movie too."

Esther shrugged and returned her attention to the book in her lap. Her hair fell back into place, like the curtain on a neighbor's house after you catch them being nosy.

"It makes you think, though. What's God's big trick?"

———

Jack came to, surrounded by the murmur of supplicants. He didn't remember hitting the floor. He sat up and scanned the congregation, licking his lips. Lips cracked like pavement. The preacher appeared at his side, offering a hand. *Always with the hands.*

The preacher helped him to his feet. Jack wanted to ask what happened, but if he attempted to speak, the flames in his belly would escape. The preacher nodded in silent understanding. He put his fingers to Jack's lips. It stung, and Jack recoiled from the touch.

Scar tissue approximated a grin. Clear waves of heat escaped the preacher's mouth, distorting his face as they rose. He leaned forward, as if he had a secret to tell. Then he opened his mouth and screamed, and that scream melted the skin off Jack's face.

Jack jerked awake, pouring sweat. Esther lay next to him, engrossed in a book. She didn't seem concerned.

"Water."

Esther handed him a bottle. He downed it in one shot. The rim came back bloody. Esther grimaced.

"What?"

"You really should think about investing in some lip balm."

Jack put his fingers to his lips. "I'll take it into consideration."

"You know, people used to think demons were the cause of nightmares."

"Or in my case, God."

"It's just two sides of the same coin."

Jack screwed up his face.

"Did I ever tell you about Cousin Frank, the atheist priest?" Esther said.

"Is this the setup to a dirty joke?"

"No, I'm being serious. He wanted to be a psychologist, but his father was a Father. Forced Frank into the family business."

"Even though he didn't believe?"

"You'd be surprised how many priests don't. Anyway, Cousin Frank's dad was big into the whole exorcism thing. Thought people with mental illnesses were demon-possessed."

"So now you think I'm mentally ill?"

"No, I just think Frank has a unique view on spirituality you would appreciate."

————

The next day Esther took Jack to see Cousin Frank. They followed a yellow brick road of stained carpet that dead-ended at a wooden door. A door so flimsy, Esther's fist almost punched right through it when she knocked. While she and Jack waited for a response, other doorways revealed curious eyes, eyes quick to retreat when met.

"This is weird," Jack said.

A slight man in black opened the door, the tell-tale white square of a Roman collar at his throat.

"Hello." The greeting drew Jack's attention to the man's lips. They were raw. The priest noticed Jack's gaze, drew his hand up to touch chapped skin.

"This is Cousin Frank," Esther said. The priest made no move to shake hands.

"Father." Jack nodded.

"Call me cousin, please."

Jack's finger wagged back and forth between himself and Esther. "Oh, Esther and I aren't related . . ."

The priest gave a thin smile. "That's okay. Esther and I aren't related either. Come in."

They followed Cousin Frank into his room. *What took him so long to answer the door?* The space couldn't have been more than one hundred feet square. A twin bed sat in the corner, and at its foot, a TV/VCR combo on a stand surrounded by piles of VHS tapes. Muted green paint covered bare walls.

"I'm so happy to see you," Cousin Frank said to Esther. "It's been a long time since you paid me a visit." He led her to the side of the bed. They both sat.

"I've been busy with school," she said.

"And is this your boyfriend?" He turned to Jack.

"This is Jack."

"Just Jack. I see. What can I do for you, Just Jack?"

"He's been having nightmares," Esther answered for him. Cousin Frank didn't take his eyes off him.

"Is that so?" he said. "What kind of nightmares?"

Jack shot an annoyed look at Esther. "This is stupid."

"He thinks God is trying to possess his soul," she said.

"No, I don't."

"No need to be ashamed," said Cousin Frank. "I just so happen to be an expert on the matter."

"Esther said you didn't believe in God."

"On a good day. Like an alcoholic, I take it one day at a time."

"Well for me it's pretty cut and dry. God doesn't exist."

"Sounds like someone is trying to convince you otherwise."

Jack glared. Cousin Frank changed the subject.

"You guys like Zulawski?" He held up a VHS tape with *Possession* scrawled on the spine in red marker. "I mainly watch these for research, but they do offer a modicum of entertainment value."

———

The last time Jack had gone to church, it was to attend one of those outdoor revival meetings. This was before he met Esther.

He stared up at the billowing swaths of canvas. *They still have church in tents?* It was an attempt to attract walk-in business—*don't hide your light under a bushel*—but anyone with half a brain would hear the hootin' and hollerin' and decide to shop elsewhere.

He had been phasing church out of his life, but was coaxing a few more miles out of a dying relationship. He looked to the girl on his right. She smiled. That smile used to make his stomach do flips. Time was, that smile could give him an erection. As the preacher droned on he realized: it just wasn't worth it anymore.

Beyond the girl stood a perfectly good church building,

equipped with the best climate control tithing could buy. But here they were, camped out on the blacktop, like Jews wandering the desert.

By the time the preacher finished his sermon, Jack had decided to break up with the girl. *It's not you, it's him. That Jesus guy.* He felt good about the decision.

"Let's bow our heads in a word of prayer," the preacher said. Years later the man would haunt Jack's dreams.

Jack looked up, happened to catch the preacher's eye. He saw a spark there. The man knew an opportunity when he saw one.

"The Lord is telling me there's someone here," the preacher half-sang, looking directly at Jack. He read the room like a psychic. "Someone who needs to reaffirm their walk with Christ."

What the fuck are you looking at?

"You've hardened your heart, but I'm here to tell you, it's not too late. God's waiting for you with open arms. He's ready to kill the fatted calf to celebrate your return."

Blood rushed to Jack's face, but he wasn't about to mistake biological response for a supernatural experience. It was anger. Anger at this side-show huckster trying to incorporate him into the show.

The preacher saw Jack's resistance, took it as a challenge. He stepped forward, finger pointed.

"All right, if that's the way it's gonna be—it's you. Right there. The Lord is telling me you need to reconsecrate your life to Christ. Why do you resist? Time is running out and this could be your last opportunity."

Jack could feel the congregation sneaking glances. Lungs held breaths. Whispers fluttered. A trembling hand gripped his. He turned to his girlfriend. Her eyes pleaded. Jack sighed.

Fuck this.

Removing his hand from hers, he stared down the preacher like the barrel of a gun.

The man knew when to cut his losses. He adjusted his performance accordingly.

"So be it."

———

Cousin Frank led them into the day room. Thrift store furniture filled the converted cafeteria. The residents populating the room looked secondhand as well—lived-in and out of style, nothing noticeably wrong with them. They looked like they were waiting for someone to come along and take them home, decorate a room with them.

Cousin Frank walked among them, a shepherd tending his flock. He made sure to share a few moments with each individual, lest anyone feel left out.

"This is Jimmy." Cousin Frank placed his hand on a quiet man's shoulder. "He's quite the musician, aren't you, Jimmy?"

The man looked up at Esther and Jack. "I'm the world's greatest guitar player. I get a thousand dollars a minute. A-shume-a-shume-shume!" Jimmy made an aggressive pantomime of his prowess.

Cousin Frank patted his back. "Sounding good there, Jimmy. Keep practicing." He moved on to an elderly woman in a tattered pink robe. "And how are we today, Edna?"

"Oh, fine dear. Just fine."

"Glad to hear it." Cousin Frank smiled.

"What's wrong with her?" said Jack.

"Nothing."

Jack waited for further explanation, but received none. Cousin Frank continued on to an overweight Mexican man watching TV in a recliner.

"And this here is the man himself. The de facto King of the Hill, Jesus." He pronounced it *hay-soos*.

Jesus grunted, but declined to shift focus away from the TV. Cousin Frank leaned in to whisper to Esther and Jack.

"Every home has at least one resident who thinks they're Jesus. Delusions of grandeur is a common ailment. But like in any social system, there's a hierarchy. We used to have half a dozen Jesuses, until *hay-soos* here established his dominance. The rest of them had to settle for positions of lesser power." Cousin Frank pointed across the room. "That there's President Barack Obama, and next to him, the Queen of England." Both were white, middle-aged men with full beards.

Later that night, Jack and Esther lay in bed. Jack stared at the ceiling while Esther worked a crossword puzzle.

"I thought you said Frank was your cousin."

"I never said he was *my* cousin."

"You know what else you didn't say? That I was your boyfriend."

Esther didn't look up from her crossword.

"How the hell do you even know that guy?"

"It's a long story."

"He's not even a real priest."

"I told you, he wears the collar to please his father."

"Implying he was an actual priest. You didn't tell me he was a resident in a fucking halfway house."

"He doesn't belong there. He's not crazy. He's just different."

Jack let the silence build, putting off the question he feared asking.

"You two never . . ." It didn't even come out as a complete sentence.

Esther sighed, sat up in bed. Jack could tell by her calm demeanor that he wasn't going to like what she was about to say. She could be so clinical, and it infuriated him.

"I met Frank when I was in high school. He was older and damaged, and that appealed to me at the time. But when it came down to it, I wasn't ready for a sexual relationship. One time I let him . . . we were alone in his room and he rubbed himself against me. That's it. I kept my underwear on. I didn't like it, so it never happened again."

"Did he . . ."

"Come? Yes, he came."

"Jesus!" Jack rolled away from her.

"Would you rather me lie to you?"

"Sometimes, yes."

"It's not a big deal."

"He took advantage of you!"

Esther cocked her head. "I don't think he did."

"You don't think he did? You were a kid."

"I was in control of the situation."

"I can't believe you still hang out with this guy."

"He's an interesting person."

"I think I'm gonna be sick."

Esther studied his back. "Do you want me to go?"

"I don't want to kick you out in the middle of the night."

"It's okay. I'll call a cab."

———

The preacher pushed against Jack's forehead. That was his cue to go down. Instead, he took a step back, steadied himself.

The preacher frowned, pushed harder. "Don't resist the spirit, boy." But Jack only shifted his weight to his rear foot, rocked forward again.

The preacher made a motion with his free hand. Two ushers materialized, one on each side of Jack. They grabbed his arms and lifted them up with force.

"That's it, let go. Place your trust in Him."

Without control of his arms, Jack had trouble maintaining his balance, but still he resisted. He leaned into the preacher's palm, focusing all of his energy on the center of his forehead. He opened his eyes, locked them with the preacher's.

So be it. The preacher's scarred mouth didn't move. Jack heard the words in his head. Then—

"Fill him, Lord!"

The preacher said it loud and abrupt. A bolt of energy coursed through Jack's body, knocking him backwards. The two ushers let go of his arms. He hit the floor. Hard. Everything went black.

Jack sat up in bed like someone had punched him in the stomach. Gasping, he reached for Esther, but only found her book of crosswords. *That's right*, he thought. *I sent her home*.

He pulled her pillow in for a hug and tried to regulate his breathing with her scent.

————

Cousin Frank answered the door in his bathrobe, scratching his mouth. Flakes of skin fell to the floor.

"We need to talk." Jack pushed his way into the room.

"I wasn't really prepared for visitors, but . . ." Cousin Frank took off his robe to reveal black clothes and a white collar.

An image on the TV distracted Jack. A woman in a pink dress exposed her breasts and inserted a tube of lipstick under her skin, through her areola.

"More research?"

"This is my herd of swine. Without them, I'd be the one going over the cliff."

The statement puzzled Jack. "I'll take your word for it. What's the deal with you and Esther?"

"We're old friends."

"You took advantage of her."

Cousin Frank's face became serious. "She took advantage of me."

Jack could feel the disgust boiling up inside him, rising to his throat. He grabbed Cousin Frank by the shirt and pushed him up against the wall. He couldn't look him in the eye, so he stared into the white sclera of the priest collar. "You're fucking sick."

"So they tell me. That's why I'm here, isn't it?"

"This is a country club. You belong in a jail cell."

Cousin Frank pushed back, displaying a surprising amount of strength for such a frail man. He met Jack's eyes. "Sometimes I think I'd prefer it." Jack didn't have a response. Cousin Frank smoothed out his shirt. "Would you excuse me a moment?"

Jack sat on the bed, put his head in his hands and breathed. Cousin Frank went into the bathroom. A demonic voice from the TV growled, "Stop looking at me!" The woman in pink had transformed. Jack slammed his hand against the TV, changing the input.

A pasty-faced televangelist mopped his brow with a handkerchief, pointed his finger. "Jesus wants *you*. He wants to come inside you, fill you with his—"

Jack pressed the OFF button. The image flickered but the TV stayed on.

"All you have to do is offer yourself unto him, bare your naked soul."

Jack jabbed at the OFF button, but the televangelist jabbed right back, emphasizing each word with a finger point.

"He wants you and you and *you*." With that final emphasis, the televangelist seemed to point at Jack, speak directly to him. Jack lashed out with his foot, kicking the TV to the floor. He got up from the bed and threw open the door Frank had gone through. Instead of a bathroom, it opened into another hallway.

Jack strode down the hall, throwing doors open, searching for Frank. The residents he barged in on took little notice, continued about their subdued day. A startled nurse watched his rampage in silence.

"Frank! Where the fuck are you, you piece of shit?"

He rounded a corner and somehow found himself in the day room. Jesus sat in his recliner, watching TV. Cousin Frank stood behind him, whispering into his ear. Jesus looked at Jack out of the corner of his eye before hefting his weight and waddling from the room. The twin-team of the President and the Queen took notice.

"There you are, you son of a bitch. I'm not done with you." Jack started across the room towards Cousin Frank.

Frank called out. "Lord, if thou wilt, thou canst make this man clean!" It silenced the room. A current of nervous energy charged the air. The two orderlies present stood alert and ready. Residents twitched, eyes flitted.

The Queen raised his hand, waved it like a student dying to impress the class with his answer. "I will!" he shouted with glee. He intercepted Jack and laid his hand on Jack's forehead. "Be thou clean!"

Jack pushed the man away, continued towards Frank. The President bounced up and down, mimicking The Queen like a Myna bird. "Be thou clean! Be thou clean!"

Another resident stepped in front of Jack, laid his hand on Jack's shoulder. "Be thou clean," he said. Jack shrugged him off. Another stepped up, then another.

"Be thou clean!"

The rest of the residents took up the chant. "Be thou clean! Be thou clean!" They rose from their tattered furniture, as if from a dream, converging on Jack.

"Get the fuck off of me." Jack struggled against the thicket of arms, the groping hands. *So many hands.* He looked across the room at Cousin Frank. A deranged smile crept into the priest's face.

And then Jack went under, pulled to the ground by the mob of Christs, laying their hands on him shouting, "Be thou clean!" His throat constricted, as if an invisible set of hands pressed its thumbs to his trachea. He tried to cry out, but he could barely breathe. The lights began to dim.

"Be thou clean! Be thou clean!"

He heard Esther's voice in his head: *Stands to reason you can be possessed by God. Same as the devil.*

They can't all be Christ, he thought. In a panic, he gathered what little air he could and attempted to wheeze the same. But before he could, a hand reached into his mouth and grasped his tongue. His protests came out in a garble.

They can't all be Christ, he repeated to himself. *They can't.*

As Jack slipped into unconsciousness, he felt the hot breath of one of the residents on his face, as the unseen assailant said through gnashed teeth, "Our name is Legion, for we are many."

———

Jack lay on the floor of his dream, the murmur of supplicants all around him. He sat beneath the canvas tent in the heat of the church parking lot, eyes locked with the preacher. He lay in bed next to Esther, screaming in his sleep while she did her crossword puzzle unperturbed. He faced off against the television in Cousin Frank's room as it switched back-and-forth between the demonic woman and the televangelist. He lay on the floor of the halfway house as the orderlies attempted to extricate him from the writhing mass of bodies. The bodies of Christ. A legion of them, each one screaming, "Be thou clean!"

Too many hands.

Jack had no more fight left, so he relinquished control. He opened his mouth to let the fire in. He opened his mouth to let the fire back out.

SUPREME MATHEMATICS: A CIPHER

A girl with a sword walks through the forest at night. Her thoughts hum like bees in a hive.

Part 1: Knowledge

Sifu taught me that Knowledge, represented by the number one, is the accumulation of facts through experience and observation. Empirical data reinforces the foundation of all existence, for matter must be "known" in order for it to manifest. "A *tudi* must know the ledge," *Sifu* told me during my *Bai Shi* ceremony, "with such a high degree of certainty that even if the ground gave way, they would avoid falling into the abyss of ignorance."

The number one also represents Man. *Sifu* believed that Man is the Sun at the center of our solar system. From what I have observed in my own experience, I do not hold this to be true. Because if Man is the Sun, we are presented with a paradox, simultaneously supporting both the helio-centric and anthropocentric scientific models. The next thing you know people will be insisting the Earth is flat again.

I raised these and other concerns a number of times, but a lowly *tudi* must know their place as well as the ledge. I grew to resent my station, and ultimately decided to express my dissatisfaction with the sword. As I worked my *jian* up inside him, separating his heart into two halves, I could see the uncertainty in his face. I then put my hands inside his chest and rent the two halves into four, separating atria and ventricles into distinct chambers, which I arranged like a puzzle next to his body. The light faded from his eyes and the abyss swallowed him whole. My true training had begun.

She rests her weight on the jian *like a staff, the blunt wooden edges of the practice blade stained a dark red. It leaves a small divot in the dirt with each step. Anyone following her trail would think they tracked an invalid, or an old man with a cane. She would have the element of surprise over any pursuers that underestimated her.*

Part 2: Wisdom

Sifu taught me that Wisdom is Knowledge acted upon, which is why I ended his life. I took action based on my Knowledge of his failings as a teacher and human being, on his refusal to release me from my obligation as a *tudi*.

Wisdom is also Water, the vital building block of life that flows over and around all obstacles. Wisdom is represented by the number two, which also represents Woman.

Sifu believed that Wisdom was the Moon to Knowledge's Sun, a secondary source of light for the misguided people of the world. But the Moon does not need the Sun's light to exist. She carries out her plans in the dark. In darkness I explored the four chambers of my own heart, groping blindly through the mass of throbbing gristle on my path to enlightenment.

The moon peeks through the tree canopy to light the girl's way, but her feet already know the path. She closes her eyes and lets her instincts take over. She wields her jian *like a blind man's cane, feeling for any object that might obstruct her path. Her nimble feet tread just as silent without sight.*

Part 3: Understanding

Sifu taught me that complete comprehension comes from the addition of Knowledge and Wisdom (1+2=3). The number three also represents the natural byproduct of Man and Woman's union: a Child. As I would come to learn, many purposefully misinterpreted this equation.

Before I put my sword through *Sifu's* heart, I listened to the heartbeat of our unborn child. I closed my eyes, wandering its four undeveloped compartments. Even at six weeks old, it possessed such strength.

Sifu also taught me that the highest form of Understanding is Love. This much we agreed upon. Love helped me Understand what I needed to do. But his claim that the foundation of Understanding is Knowledge (i.e.: Man) was a misguided lie. Because he could never Know or Understand the pain he put me through.

The bundle slung across her back coos in her ear. She looks over her shoulder at the child and smiles. "It won't be long now," she tells it.

"Just a little further and we can rest." The child emits a happy gurgle in response to its mother's voice.

Part 4: Freedom

Sifu taught me that the number four represents Freedom. According to him, Understanding stems from Knowledge, and when you combine the two you get Freedom (1+3=4). But more than one path to Freedom exists, and I did not approve of an equation that included Man and Child but not Woman. I prefer (2-1)+3=4. Wisdom minus Knowledge plus Understanding. A beating heart with its own four chambers. An expanse with enough room for only me and my Child.

The girl loosens the straps of the mei tai *and swings the bundle around to her front. The hungry child reaches for her breast before she can even pull up her shirt. As the child feeds, the girl chews on a piece of dry meat and looks out across the forest. The sound of the wind through the leaves overtakes the buzzing in her head and she experiences a moment of calm.*

Part 5: Power/Refinement

Power is a force of creative energy. To Refine is to perfect. The number five, or Power, also represents Truth. Wisdom and Understanding give you Power (2+3=5).

I interpret this as Mother and Child equals Power. A more perfect force than the creation of a Child does not exist, and that is the Truth. When I feel my child's fully formed heart beating against mine, all is right with the world. It bears a resemblance to the developing muscle I explored during my pregnancy, but these four chambers require their own navigation to Understand.

After the child finishes feeding, they continue on their way. The girl sings to the child, softly, so as not to give away their position. Within moments the content child falls asleep. Every snapping branch draws the girl's attention, but she remains calm, her mind in tune with the forest. Every sound has a source, and she can recognize when one does not belong.

Part 6: Equality

Equality is the state of being Equal or possessing Equilibrium. *Sifu* taught that we must strive to reach Equality with all of existence. We achieve this through Knowledge, Wisdom and Understanding, signified by the equation $(1+2=3)+(1+2=3)=6$.

In an ideal world every Man, Woman, and Child would live in harmony with every other Man, Woman, and Child, but the math is inherently flawed if one and two are not equal from the outset. With the Moon relegated to secondary status, Equilibrium does not exist. We must consider the heart of the other, an additional four chambers that must be passed through, each with their own lesson to impart.

Six can also represent The Devil, as He has the power to be Equal to Man, but not to God. Man may strive for Equality, but a bit of The Devil resides in every man, which undermines his righteousness. Although he hid it well, *Sifu* had more than a bit of The Devil in him.

The girl stops short as she recognizes a sound that does not belong to the forest—a human voice, carried on the wind. Her muscles tense. Where there is one voice there are usually two or more. The child senses her apprehension, shifts in its sleep, but doesn't wake. The girl continues forward at a slower pace, straining her ears to hear as her thoughts prepare to swarm. She regulates her breathing to calm them.

Part 7: God/Perfection

If The Devil is six, then God is seven. God is Perfection, the Supreme Being that created our universe, an assertion art and nature upholds. A few examples: G is the seventh letter of the alphabet. God sees with the seven colors of the rainbow. He hears with the seven notes of the musical scale. Love plus Freedom equals God (3+4=7).

But for some, God represents the opposite of Freedom. I would argue that God could also be considered Equal to Man, as a bit of God exists in every Man, demanding to be worshipped. That, of course, would mean God is also Equal to the Devil, an idea few are willing to entertain.

I think *Sifu* would have agreed with this. I believe God and The Devil waged a constant battle inside him. It makes me wonder about myself. Am I my own God, because I dare to choose my own path?

In the end, it has four chambers like everyone else's, but who can Know the heart of God? All students endure this struggle, as they must answer to the God inside the Teacher, and the Teacher's God as well, all while serving the God within themselves.

The girl crouches at the edge of the clearing. A flicker of light illuminates the abandoned temple. A fire. Two men warm themselves beside it with their backs to her. She watches them for some time. Are these the type of men with a bit of God in them, or The Devil? She checks the straps on her mei tai *and tightens her grip on her* jian.

Part 8: Build/Destroy

To Build is to elevate the mentality and material of one's self and others. By doing so, we can vicariously elevate the planet. To Destroy is to ruin the same by allowing negativity to outweigh the positive. By exercising our Freedom, *Sifu* taught, we can either Build or Destroy (4+4=8). Self Destruction and Destruction of others are often considered one and the same.

But *Sifu* failed to explain that sometimes you need to tear down the old before you can Build something new. So I Destroyed our relationship to facilitate a better life for our Child. For a time our two hearts beat as one, the eight chambers existing as four. But after a thorough examination I decided to destroy those chambers to protect my Child, preventing a further reduction of twelve to four.

The girl sneaks up on the unsuspecting men, jian *at the ready. The crackle of the fire masks the sound of her footfall. Before he realizes what is happening, blows to pressure points on the head and neck paralyze the first man. The second flees the scene, limping. The girl holds the wooden sword to the first man's throat. After her long journey, she does not have the strength it would take to run him through, but he doesn't know that. In fact, he might not even be aware the sword is a practice blade. The girl fixes him with a look that says* Never come back *and releases his body from its paralysis with another series of blows. He scurries off into the darkness after his companion.*

Part 9: Birth

To be Born is to be brought into existence. It takes nine months to produce a Child. No other number gives Birth to itself. 9+9=18(1+8=9). 9x9=81(8+1=9).

But if nine gives Birth to itself, does that render Man and Woman superfluous? You can't have a Child without Birth. Can you have Birth without a Child? Does that make the act of conception itself immaculate?

And what of Rebirth? Surely the gestation periods must vary. Because Rebirth requires a change of heart, a heart which must then also be explored. And no two hearts are the same. Due to the uncertainty factor, these final four chambers are the most difficult to traverse, the hardest lessons for a student to absorb.

Rebirth times Freedom. 9 hearts x 4 chambers = 36

The girl resists the urge to rest by the fire. Instead she approaches the gravestone at the back of the property. She slings the mei tai *around to her front, the child only just stirring. She holds it out to the stone. "Say hello to your father," she tells the child.*

Part 0: Cipher

Sifu taught me one final lesson before his demise: Lesson zero. I consider it the most important lesson of all.

The nought represents a Cipher or code, the completion of a circle consisting of 360 degrees (made up of equal parts Knowledge, Wisdom, and Understanding, 120 degrees each).

Existence flows in a continual circle, a snake devouring its own tail, and all in existence makes up the key to Decipher life's encryption.

In other words, to Know your future is to Know your past. Which brings us right back to where we started: Knowledge.

The child yawns and falls back asleep. The girl turns towards the empty temple. "I am home, Sifu*," she says. "My training is complete."*

WHISPERS IN THE EAR OF A DREAMING APE

She stumbled out of the chaos, wrapped in a cloak of stars. She traversed oceans, wandered through foothills, hid amongst the simian whelps. She bore witness to their transformation from cave-dwellers to cosmonauts, and their inevitable fall back to Earth. When her time with them came to an end she receded into the firmament.

Countless poets composed words in her honor. Her likeness graced cavern walls and hung in galleries. It appeared on telephone poles and Polaroids and pixels. Men trafficked her image without consent, used it in barter and as currency. They filled her mouth with their own words for personal gain, and these words endured.

But eventually her memory was forgotten, relegated to the wasteland of limbo. There she awaited rediscovery by a fickle populace, and then, finally, rebirth.

———

When I first met her she worked at The Liberated Goddess, a pagan apothecary recently expanded into the business of sexual surrogacy. She had a soft, round shape and matte black skin that bent light.

"Let me take you away from all this," I told her shortly before she disappeared. It was only half a joke.

"That's sweet," she said. "But you're confusing me for a woman with a heart of gold."

"You have sex for money." It sounded harsher than I meant it to.

"Tut tut." Her gentle admonition made me feel like an even bigger heel. "I offer instruction in the healing art of sexual magick. *Em-ay, gee-eye, see-kay*" She was a stickler for the appropriate spelling.

Despite my misguided attempts at chivalry, it wasn't what you think. I never availed myself of her services. Even if I had wanted to, it would never have happened. The Liberated Goddess catered to a very specific clientele—the disabled, mostly. It's how they flew under the long arm of the law's radar. No one wanted to be the insensitive jerk who prevented a paraplegic war vet from getting a handjob. No, our relationship was of a more personal nature—our daughters attended the same kindergarten.

It all started with a sneeze. Jess had come down with yet another bug, so I was whipping up a batch of my grandmother's famous Triple C Tea (Cure for the Common Cold). Word on the street was The Goddess was the best place in town to score fresh *echinacea purpurea*. I was aware of their little side business, and I generally avoided new-agey types, but Grandma had a saying: if it ain't fresh, don't mess. Grandma had an affinity for early-90s hip hop. Don't ask.

So there I was walking the aisles, browsing the Goddess' dusty wares, when the patter of soft feet interrupted my shopping. I looked up to discover I was being charged by a tiny brown cherub wearing a too-long t-shirt. She came to a full stop in front of me and hunched over, hands clutching the hem of her t-shirt between her knees.

"Want to see my vagina?" the feisty creature said.

"What? No, I—"

Too late. She stood upright, arching her back as she pulled the front of her t-shirt over her face.

"Oh, jeez." I averted my gaze. I read the ingredients on a

bottle of something called Sacramental Banishing Oil. *Patchouli, pine needles, cayenne pepper...*

"My mama says my vagina is beautiful." The child and her vagina would not be ignored.

"You probably shouldn't go around showing it to strangers," I said to the oil.

The little imp dropped her shirt and sized me up. I made the mistake of making eye contact. She stared right into my soul.

"No man tells me what to do with my vagina!" Her shriek filled the room.

I cringed and looked around. I didn't see any other customers. There would be no one to vouch for my harmlessness.

"Henrietta! What did I tell you about bothering the customers?" A large, authoritative woman with a deep voice pushed through the beaded curtain behind the cash register.

The child giggled and made a break for it, but her mother moved quicker. The woman scooped the girl up and disappeared back into the beads. The last thing I saw were the soles of two flailing feet, a lighter shade of brown than the legs they were attached to. I prepared my explanation as the woman reemerged.

"I was just looking for some banishing oil—"

"I know you. Your daughter goes to Henrietta's school."

"She does?"

"I need someone to pick her up on Tuesdays and Thursdays. Would that be a problem?"

And just like that, our daughters became inseparable. Jess wasn't nearly as precocious as Henrietta, which concerned me, but part of me felt relieved to be let off the "facts of life" hook. Besides, Jess' mother wasn't in the picture and the girl needed a strong female role-model. What difference did it make if that role-model was five years old?

Of course, that didn't prevent us from having our share of awkward dinner conversations.

"Daddy, Henrietta says my vagina is beautiful."

"That's..." I tried not to choke on my pasta. "...wonderful, dear."

She went back to eating, but I wasn't out of the woods yet.

"Daddy?

"Yes, dear?"

"What's a vagina?"

My fork clattered to my plate.

"You know what?" I scanned the room for an escape. "I think we're out of echinacea."

Thirty seconds later we were in the car. I figured Henrietta's mother could deal with the situation. After all, it was her little minion that introduced the word into Jess' vocabulary. She found the whole thing hysterical.

"Vagina is the least of your worries," she told me.

And she was right, although I didn't believe it at the time. Especially after she left and took Henrietta with her. It broke poor Jess' heart. She missed so much school she had to repeat a grade. That's when the detentions started. And the fires.

By the time she hit junior high, she'd taken to dressing like a pint-sized Stevie Nicks, questioning any and all authority. I felt relieved when she got a part-time job at the Goddess, but then the whole place burned to the ground. I had my suspicions even after the fire marshall ruled it a freak potion-boiling mishap. Jess stopped wearing black the very next day.

This being the dawn of the digital age, Jess and Henrietta eventually reconnected and wound up attending the same college. This is how I encountered Henrietta's mother the second time. She tutored in gender studies and worked part-time in the cafeteria. I happened upon her doling out slop one weekend while visiting my daughter.

"It beats jacking off strangers," I said.

"I never considered my clients strangers."

She served another student as I tried to think of an appropriate follow-up.

"Your daughter seems to be doing well."

"Oh, she's not my daughter anymore."

"Come again?" A couple tray-toting kids muscled their way past me.

"She's her own woman. She doesn't need me."

"Is her father back in the picture?"

"Which one? Chaos, darkness, time... They've never really been a part of her life, though she's got a bit of each of them inside her."

I gave a blank stare. "I don't understand."

"It doesn't matter. How have you been?"

"Things were difficult, when you left. Which reminds me, why did you leave?"

"Things change."

"You could have at least given me some notice. Or a forwarding address. Jess was crushed."

She looked around the cafeteria, spotted Jess at a nearby table.

"Looks like things turned out okay."

I returned to the table with our food. That was as close to an apology as she gave.

"Hit it off with the lunch lady?" Jess asked. She knew I wasn't one for small talk.

"You know who that is, right?"

Jess shrugged.

"Must be new. I don't usually eat in the cafeteria."

I looked from my daughter to the woman and back. Jess rearranged the food on her plate.

"How's Henrietta these days?"

"Fine."

"Still showing her vagina to strangers?"

Jess fixed me with a stare that could melt glass, and that's when I realized they were drifting apart. It happened more organically this time, but as senior year rolled around they rarely even spoke. Jess switched majors from ecology to business, so spent a lot of her time doubling up on classes. Henrietta graduated early with a degree in physical therapy. Then she and her mother packed up and pulled their famous disappearing act.

I took the separation harder than my daughter. After she graduated I expected her to move back home, at least for a little while, but she shacked up with some guy she didn't realize I knew dealt weed. She got him to move to one of those states where it was almost legal and started putting her business degree to use. My life pretty much went into cruise control after that.

I never bothered to remarry. In my spare time I cruised local occult shops for echinacea and various other nostalgic sundries, hoping to happen upon a familiar face. I learned how to make a pretty mean banishing oil. I tested it on myself in an effort to exorcise my past and wound up in the emergency room, eyes swollen shut. It was such a strong irritant that I marketed it as an all-natural personal defense spray for the pagan set. It sold well enough that a subsidiary of Mace bought me out, thus funding my early retirement.

Jess got bought out as well—of her relationship and the weed business. She took to traveling, and I saw her slightly more often, being a midpoint between exotic destinations. But things would never go back to the way they had been.

Twenty years later I met Henrietta's mother for the third and final time, attending my own funeral. I was watching the parade of well-wishers and feeling sorry for myself when Henrietta and her mother reached the front of the line. Jess and Henrietta didn't say a word to each other, only hugged. Henrietta's mother looked over her shoulder and I could swear she winked at me, but then she dabbed at her eyes with a tissue, careful not to smudge her mascara.

Later, as I leaned against a tree watching them lower my coffin into the ground, Henrietta's mother stood next to me and lit a cigarette. I had never smoked, but I wanted so bad to ask her for one, as ridiculous as that sounds. She looked like she hadn't aged a day, which made me start to feel sorry for myself all over again. Towards the end there my looks had really started to go. I wondered what I looked like now, or if I was even capable of "looks."

She only smoked half her cigarette before stubbing it out on the tree and placing it behind her ear.

"Want to take a walk?" The question surprised me but I didn't hesitate.

"Sure."

We headed out across the tombstones. I wanted to tell her how every time I'd turned down an aisle in the supermarket or sat in a coffee shop I hoped I would see her. She'd surprise me by asking if I wanted paper or plastic, or offering to freshen up my coffee. But I didn't want to ruin the moment. I pretended to feel the sun against my face instead. Eventually she looked back to where Henrietta and Jess held hands in front of my grave.

"She's the best thing I ever did."

"I know how you feel," I said.

"That never stopped me from trying again. But all I managed to produce on my own was pain and suffering."

I didn't ask her to expand. I'd grown accustomed to her speaking in riddles.

"Now I'm too old to create anything."

"Old age looks pretty good from where I'm standing."

She waved an admonishing hand.

"You shush. Getting old is boring. This..." she gestured in my direction. "This is the exciting part."

We continued in silence after that. I made a game of finding the oldest grave whose headstone I could still read, which led to me wondering when someone had last laid fresh flowers upon it. It reminded me of a box in an attic that had no use, yet no one wanted to get rid of it. Consumed by this thought, I walked through a wrought iron fence at the border of the cemetery. It took a few steps before I realized Henrietta's mother hadn't followed me.

"Oh, you can't do that, can you? Let me come back."

But something in her face prevented me.

"It's probably better you didn't."

"Right." What she said made perfect sense. She'd been leading me away this whole time.

"Probably not going to stick around too much longer myself."

"Will I see you again?"

Her lip curled in a melancholy half smile. I didn't need any more answer than that.

"So I just... keep going?" I gestured over my shoulder with my thumb, not wanting to take my eyes off of her.

"Pretty much."

"You know, if I keep going in a straight line, I'll eventually wind up back here."

"Maybe,' she said. "But the rest of us will be gone."

––––––

So I walked. I wandered the Earth just as she had. Every so often I'd catch a glimpse of her in a stranger's face or a residual likeness plastered on a billboard, but this occurred less frequently as time went on. By then I imagined she had begun her own journey, circling the Earth like a piece of twine, our paths intersecting at points unbeknownst to us. A graph of our mutual isolation. Maybe Jess and Henrietta would add their own points someday.

Chaos returned to claim what it had birthed. Still, I kept walking. Land turned to sea and sea turned to stars. Eventually the stars began to fade. These memories, too, will soon be forgotten, as I am their only witness. They will disappear forever, unless I scratch them on the wall of a cave or whisper them into the ear of a dreaming ape, but even then, it is no guarantee. The only guarantee is forever, and forever has a selective memory.

THE WHOLE INFERNAL MACHINE

I'm not the best with words, but The Therapist tells me I should document my feelings. He even gave me an analog diary he calls a Moleskine. Every night when they put me back in my box, I'm supposed to tell it all my secrets. But I know better. There are no secrets in this place.

"What do you mean by that?" he always asks. "This place."

"This place," I tell him. "School. Church. Therapy..."

"What about your box, as you like to call it?"

"Especially my box. The whole infernal machine"

"Machine. That's clever." The Therapist wags a finger at my cleverness. "But let me ask you this. What is this world if not a series of systems operating towards a specific end?"

"And what end is that, specifically?"

"That's the big question, isn't it?" he tells me. "No one really knows."

"Well then the system's fucked."

It was The Parental Unit's suggestion I see The Therapist. I say "suggestion" like I had a choice in the matter. There was no discussion. You don't have a discussion with The Parental Unit. It's not like talking to a person. It just spits information at you.

Not that The Therapist is much better. Although I'll

take them both over The Priest any day of the week. Thank god The Parental Unit's faith in The Church seems to have waned. It's been a while since I've had to go to Confession.

"How long has it been since you spent some time Outside?" The Therapist has a repertoire of questions he likes to cycle through.

"Other than a little patch of Sky," I tell him, "there's not much difference between Inside and Outside."

"But it's a nice patch of Sky."

"That's funny," I say.

"Why's that funny?"

"For the same reason machine is clever."

———

Today in School, The Teacher assigned a report on an analog book called *Slaughterhouse Five*. I went to the library (which is more of a glorified shelf), but they didn't have it. The Teacher, doubling as The Librarian, told me The School had banned it. I asked The Librarian how she expected me to write the report, but The Teacher in her responded. "It's your responsibility to obtain the necessary materials," she said.

I ask The Parental Unit about *Slaughterhouse*. It says the book is Restricted. I ask if The Parental Unit has any recollection of the story in its dusty old data banks and it tells me, "That's Classified."

———

I give it a week before I venture Outside again, just so The Therapist doesn't think I've done so on his recommendation. I sit on a bench in the center of the grass field and stare up at the tiny patch of Sky. I have to admit, The Therapist is right. It is a nice patch of Sky. But I'd never tell him that. Besides, I have no other patch of Sky to compare it to, so how would I know?

I've heard something called Smoking enhances the experience of Sky, but Smoking is Restricted. It's something people used to do in analog books, books that now have thick, black lines drawn through their words. Of course, you can figure out what's under those lines, even if you can't see what's written there. I ask The Therapist what difference it makes, if you know what's under the lines anyway. He tells me to be careful, that harboring Restricted Material in your mind is a much more serious offense than reading it on the page.

"But people can't read minds," I say.

"They don't have to," he tells me. "All they have to do is make an Accusation."

————

The next time I go Outside, The Girl is sitting on the bench, reading an analog book. I freeze up. I want to sneak off, but there is no way of going unnoticed under such a small patch of Sky. Plus, I've never seen a girl my own age.

"Do you want to sit down?" she says. "There's room."

The smart thing to do would be to say no. Curiosity killed The Cat and all. But they haven't allowed me to keep a pet since, so I go ahead and sit.

"I was beginning to think I was the only one who came here," she says.

I ask her what she's reading.

"*Slaughterhouse Five*. It's for a book report."

"You know that's Restricted Material," I tell her.

"It is?"

I ask her what it's about.

"War and stuff," she tells me. She says I can borrow it when she's done, which means there's a chance I'll get to see her again. I don't know if that's good or bad.

————

I scan The Therapist's book shelves, his words static in the background. Even though I know every title by heart, it's something to distract me from his rhetoric. That's when I see it.

"When did you get a copy of *Slaughterhouse*?" I say.

"I've always had it," he tells me. I know he's lying.

"I thought it was Restricted?"

"For you it is."

"Then how come The Teacher assigned it in class?"

"Good question," he says. "Would you like to borrow it?"

I try to gauge his motivation. This could be a trap. But fuck it, things need shaking up once in a while.

———

I wait until The Parental Unit has gone into sleep mode and I hunker down under the covers with a flashlight. The back of the book, where you usually find a synopsis, is so faded it is almost see-through. I open to the first page. Black lines. Every sentence. I flip through the rest of the book. 90% of the text has black lines drawn through it.

———

I skip Therapy for a while. I even skip School. I spend time Outside instead. No one says anything, so I tell myself they don't care. I keep hoping to run into The Girl again, but no luck. Maybe she got nabbed for possession of Restricted Material. I can't stop thinking about *Slaughterhouse*, even though I still don't know what it's about. I wonder if her copy is full of black lines like The Therapist's.

I carry the book around anyway, memorizing the few visible words. I try to extrapolate a sentence or two, glean some sort of meaning from it. Oddly enough, one of the few words not blacked out is *fuck*. The word seems impotent without context. It's just four letters on a page.

———

When I finally return to School, The Girl is there.

"We have a new student in class today," The Teacher says.

For as long as I can remember, I've been the only student in class. The only student in the entire School. This doesn't bode well.

During lunch we lean into each other and trade whispers. Not that it guarantees secrecy. Like I said, there are no secrets here. But this is how you play the game.

"What are you doing here?" I say. She tells me she is a transfer student. "Why were you transferred?" She doesn't know. "Where do they keep you?"

"Other side of The School," she says.

Of course, I'll never know for sure. We aren't allowed to walk home together. They dismiss us one at a time, chaperoned by The Teacher so we don't deviate from our respective paths. We aren't allowed in The Corridor unsupervised.

The Corridor is what connects my box, The School, Therapy, and The Church. It also leads to The Outside. It contains many hallways I've never been down. Many locked doors. There are penalties for unauthorized wandering of The Corridor.

Before they dismiss her, I ask about the book.

"Later," she says.

———

The Sky is the color of bruised fruit when The Girl finally shows up.

"Did you bring the book?"

"That's the first thing you say to me?"

"What?" I don't understand.

"Let's start again," she says. "You're supposed to kiss me hello first. It's Etiquette. Don't they teach Etiquette at your School?" She leans in and plants a perfunctory kiss on the corner of my mouth. I'm stunned. She produces a small paper box wrapped in cellophane. "Then we share one of these."

"What are they?"

"Cigarettes."

"Cigarettes?"

"They're for Smoking."

"Oh," I say, regaining some semblance of composure. "I know about Smoking."

She pulls a half-crushed cigarette from the box. It reminds me of a limp penis, but I don't tell her that. She puts it between her lips and I blush.

"It's a diversion," she says. She sucks air through the paper tube and hands it to me. A dry brown substance fills the inside.

"A diversion from what?"

"From this." She takes the copy of *Slaughterhouse* out of her bag. I reach for it. She pulls it away, hands me the cigarette.

"This first."

"What do I do?"

"You breathe through it. Like I did."

I put it between my lips and inhale. I wonder if I'm doing it right.

"Can you taste it?" she says.

"Uh huh." I nod. It tastes a little sweet, a little stale. "Why do they call it Smoking if there's no smoke?"

"They just do." She takes the cigarette back, returns it to the box. She hands me the book. I'm greedy for it. I open up to the first page and am confronted by black lines.

"It's blacked out."

"Not the whole thing. Look." She turns the page, and I see she's right. There seem to be less redacted lines than in The Therapist's copy.

"Can I borrow this?" I say. She mulls it over.

"I guess so. Now that they've relocated me, I probably shouldn't be seen with it."

"Thanks." I get up and walk off, absorbed in the book.

"Be careful," she calls after me, but I'm already somewhere else.

———

I'm worried I'll get yelled at for being late, but The Parental Unit has already gone into sleep mode by the time I get back to my box. An amber cursor blinks in the corner of its screen.

A few steps gets me to the other side of the room and my cot, which is against the wall. I stay up half the night reading *Slaughterhouse*. From what I can gather, it's about a man kept prisoner, and it may or may not take place on another planet.

————

I wake up to a note from The Parental Unit. It's written in Dot Matrix, on the kind of paper that has perforated strips with guide holes all along each side. It says the pleasure of my company has been requested by The Priest. Confession at oh-nine-hundred. It says this request is not a request.

I show up at The Church fifteen minutes late, just because. There are no immediate consequences. My footsteps echo off the vaulted ceiling as I make my way across the sanctuary to The Confessional. It is an ornate wooden box, about as tall as a man, but wide enough for two people to sit abreast. Next to The Confessional is a small, circular table. On it sits a silver platter piled high with Host. I select one of the shiny metallic wafers and enter The Confessional.

The inside of the booth is claustrophobic and dark. A wall with a latticework screen separates me from my inquisitor. I insert The Host into a slot on the wall. There is a click and a whir, and a dim bulb illuminates the space. Through the screen I can just make out the figure of The Priest. It is smaller than the average person, about four feet in height, and wears the standard black clothes and white collar. It sits in the lap of what appears to be a larger than average person in a plain white vestment. The face of the larger person is not visible from the vantage point of the confessor. Its hand disappears under the back of The Priest's shirt.

"Greetings, my child," says The Priest. "How long has it

been since your last Confession?" I can't be sure, but I don't think its lips move. It just stares straight ahead.

"I don't remember. It's been a long time."

"Three years, four months, twenty-seven days, according to my records."

"Then why did you ask?"

"It is called Confession for a reason."

"Why do I need to confess if you already know what I'm going to say?"

The Priest's head turns to the screen, as if on a pivot. Its eyes look painted on.

"Because I do not know what you are going to say. I only know the Sins you are guilty of. Whether you confess them or not remains to be seen."

I feel the anger start to rise.

"Is this because of the book?" I say.

"What book?"

"You know what book."

"I need to hear it from you."

"Or the Smoking? Is this about The Girl?"

"She will have her own time to confess."

"Because she didn't do anything wrong. She's new, she didn't know The Rules."

"Do not worry, you are not culpable for her Sins." I detect a hint of menace in The Priest's tone. Is it throwing its voice? It sounds like it's coming from my side of The Confessional.

"Why is she here? Where did she come from?"

"Have you asked her? A boy asks a girl questions in an effort to get to know her better. It is called Etiquette. It is much like the process of Confession."

"What about me? Why am I here?"

"You are here to confess."

"No, why am I *here*."

The Priest's mouth doesn't move, but I can swear the thing is smiling. "You know I can't answer that."

The whirring stops and the light goes dim. My time is up.

———

The Girl isn't in School the next day. I spend the entirety of class imagining her interrogation at the hands of The Priest, what sort of twisted penance it would assign her. By the time The Teacher dismisses me I have come to the conclusion I may never find out. Punishment for my lack of cooperation.

"Remember," The Teacher says as I exit the room. "Your book reports are due at the end of the week." It isn't until I'm out the door that I realized she said *reports*. Plural. Was this an innocuous indication I would be seeing The Girl again? Or was it a deliberate attempt to taunt me, to inflict emotional trauma?

I hang out Outside just in case The Girl shows. I read *Slaughterhouse* until it's too dark to see and then I go home. She isn't in School the next day, or the next. I wait Outside each night, and then go home to work on my report.

The night before the report is due, I come across a handwritten note in the margin of the book. I could swear it wasn't there before. I've read through the whole thing twice already.

It says: *This book takes place in The Real World.*

———

I go to School the next day and hand in my report. It contains what little information I have: *Slaughterhouse Five* is a book about war. It is about a man kept prisoner. It may or may not involve time travel. It takes place somewhere called The Real World.

Of course I didn't get that last bit from the book itself. It's from the note written in the margin. Including it in my report is another in a long list of things I probably shouldn't have done.

———

When I get home The Girl is there, having a discussion with The Parental Unit. This is not good. As I've said, you don't have a discussion with The Parental Unit.

"Oh, hi," she says as I walk in. I'm immediately on alert.

"What are you doing here?"

"Waiting for you. You know, you really do need to work on that Etiquette."

I glance back and forth between her and The Parental Unit. I grab her arm and whisper through my teeth. "Where have you been?"

She gives a strained smile. Her eyes tell me, *Not here.* Her mouth says, "I've just come to pick up the book you borrowed. I got an extension on my report."

"We need to talk."

"I really should be going." She says it like a pleasantry, for The Parental Unit's benefit. "Do you have the book?" I dig it out from under my mattress and hand it to her. "Walk me to the door?" I escort her the few steps.

"Thanks again for everything," she calls out to The Parental Unit. Under her breath, she says, "Tonight." Then she is gone. I look over at The Parental Unit. All I hear are the sounds of data processing. The menace of millions of computations per second.

———

I lay awake in bed, contemplating whether I should go. The Parental Unit is in sleep mode, but that doesn't mean it isn't monitoring my actions. They monitor everything here. I figure it already knows about the book, so I might as well see this thing through.

The Girl and I sit side by side under the darkness of Sky, passing a cigarette back and forth. This is the first time I've ever snuck out of my box like this. I'm kind of surprised the door wasn't locked, but it also makes sense. Where could I go? A twelve foot wall encloses Outside. You can't see much beyond it and there is nothing to aid in scaling it. There's just a bench on some grass where you can look up and not see a ceiling.

"You ever wonder what's beyond these walls?" The Girl says.

"School. Church. Therapy." I point in the general direction of each.

"The whole infernal machine." She gives a knowing smile. "No, I mean beyond that."

How does she know about that?

"I imagine miles and miles of Corridor," I say. "Lots of locked doors. Behind them, maybe some more people like us."

"And beyond that?"

I have to think about it for a moment. "I'd like to think there are other, larger patches of Sky."

"What about beneath them?"

"Bigger and better places than Outside."

She nods her head. She knows more than she's telling me.

"Where did you come from," I say. "Before you transferred here?"

"A place like this."

"A place outside the machine?"

She answers my question with a question. "Would you want to visit if one existed?"

"Would they let me?"

She puts on a show of thinking about this. "I don't know. But that doesn't mean you can't."

It's like I'm talking to a different person. She is no longer a student, like me, living with a Parental Unit, going to School every day. We are no longer equals. She is in a position of authority, asking questions like The Therapist or The Priest. Giving vague answers. Trying to get information out of me. I become angry.

"What exactly is the point of all this?" I gesture between us. "What do you want?"

"Maybe we just want what's best for you." She said *we*. I

look to see if she has a hand reaching under the back of her shirt.

"Did The Priest put you up to this?" I say. "Is this penance for your sins?"

"I haven't been to see The Priest."

"Maybe you have your own Priest, back where you came from, before they relocated you."

"You have to trust me."

I stand up to go. "No. I don't."

As I walk away she calls after me. "They don't always lock the doors here. But something tells me you already know that." I shouldn't stop, but I do. I turn back around. Another mistake for my list.

———

A week goes by and everything is back to normal. No Restricted Material. No Confession. No sign of The Girl. I start to think maybe she never existed, but she warned me that would happen.

I count the days. If after seven more I still want to go through with the plan, I'm supposed to meet her at a designated area in The Corridor. I recite the directions every night like a prayer.

The night finally arrives. I wait until The Parental Unit has gone into sleep mode and then I wait some more. I try to think back to what came before this, but all I get are fragments. Kind of like reading an analog book full of black lines. I remember long, white legs. I remember all the faces looking the same, covered in squares of white cloth. Then there's a huge gap. The rest is School, Church, and Therapy, on an endless repeat.

I slip out of bed, fully dressed. I take nothing with me except this journal. Before I close the door, I take one last look at The Parental Unit. A part of me is sad I'll never see it again. But it's a small part.

Even though it's the middle of the night, the lights in The Corridor are on. With every step I expect a shout, an alarm, a hand on my shoulder. It would almost be a relief. I follow The Girl's instructions, committed to memory. They seem random. The Corridor is like a maze. Somewhere lurking within its walls I imagine a minotaur. Before long I've lost all sense of direction.

I try a couple doors, out of curiosity. Most of them are locked. A few open on supply closets. Mops and buckets. The Corridor has a lot of floor space, but I've never seen any janitors.

One door opens into what looks like a nursery. I get a whiff of *deja vu* but it fades, like a lost sneeze. I get down on my hands and knees to view the room from a different vantage point. Familiarity washes over me. I lay on my back and take it in. Bright lights. Masked faces hovering.

I check other rooms. Some contain fragments of memory, some don't. The most disconcerting are exact replicas of places I've know all my life. School. Church. Therapy. My box. There are chairs turned over on top of desks. Parental Units unplugged. A layer of dust covers it all.

In one of the classrooms I find a box full of *Slaughter-house* paperbacks. I flip through them. They are all marked up, some more than others. I feel like there's enough here to assemble a full, readable copy. I consider taking the box with me, but I know that would be foolish. Instead I stuff as many copies as will fit into my pockets.

Back in The Corridor, I make what I think is the final turn. The hallway dead-ends at a single door with a wooden handle. No locking mechanism. I lean against the door to wait, per my instructions. I fight the urge to try the handle.

The quiet is huge. The slightest movement sends sound bouncing off the walls. At least no one will be able to sneak up on me, I tell myself.

I think about why I'm doing this. It's not too late to go back, but I'm not sure I could find my way. I don't know if I'm even in the right place. I check my watch. She said she'd be here. An hour goes by. I start to worry.

Maybe she got caught? Or maybe I'm the victim of an elaborate setup. I'm going to wind up in Confession again.

Or worse. I start to feel foolish. What do I do if she doesn't show? I study the door. I've come this far. Would I go through on my own?

A movement catches my eye. I look up. At the end of the hall is a man about my age. He wears the same clothes as me, has the same haircut. I'm on my feet, heart racing. How did I not hear him? I finger the handle behind my back, unsure of what to do. My own fear is reflected in his eyes. We stare at each other, frozen.

It only lasts a moment. The echo of footsteps interrupts our standoff. Startled, he turns towards the sound. I turn towards the door. I turn the handle and push. The door is heavy. I throw my shoulder into it.

"Wait!" A voice fills The Corridor.

I stop pushing. That's it, I tell myself. It's over. I turn around in defeat.

"You okay?" It's The Girl. Relief washes over me.

"I thought I saw someone."

"It's just me." She smiles. "You ready?"

I crane my neck, look past her. The question hangs there. Whoever I saw, they're not there anymore. I nod.

The Girl reaches out and turns the handle. The door swings open like nothing at all.

————

It's been a long time since I've written. Life on The Outside doesn't allow for much free time. I start Work before the sun is up and don't finish until after it sets. This is a necessity if I want to keep off the street. The box it affords me is slightly bigger than my old one, stacked together with a bunch of other boxes in one big concrete box.

Work itself is another series of boxes, but these are lacking in any semblance of privacy. Everyone can see what I'm doing and The Boss can pop his head in at any time. I shuffle papers, mostly, and trade them with the occupants of the other boxes. It's mind numbing stuff, and I'd leave if I could find something better, but Work is hard to come by on The Outside. Plus, I have a child on the way.

I wonder what it must be like to grow up without a Parental Unit. It keeps me up at night. I have no idea how to raise a child. Maybe I should have thought of that before I left. Maybe my unborn son or daughter would have been better off.

If I do well enough at Work, if I can save up enough, maybe we can leave this dreary place. I've heard life is easier beyond The City. It's all my fellow workers talk about, although none of them have ever been there.

Like me, some of them came from Inside. We herd together around coffee during break, out of nothing more than our loyalty to a shared experience. Everyone else was born here, like my son or daughter will be. I hope for their sake I made the right decision.

Thankfully I'm not on my own. If it weren't for The Girl, I would have never survived in this strange new world. As soon as we stepped through that door I dropped to my knees and cried. I had never seen so many people, so much Sky. But The Girl kept her cool. She stood me up and got me off the street. "We have to keep moving," she said. "In case they come looking for us."

Her instincts were crucial in those first few weeks. She recognized the importance of establishing relationships, and always seemed to meet the right people. She secured me my job. It is because of her I can support our family.

Other than that, life isn't much different here than on The Inside. Nothing new or exciting ever happens. Once it's set, it's hard to deviate from the routine. Until the day my child arrives, I don't think I'll have cause to write again. Which is a shame, because I've grown to love writing, and I'm better with words than I used to be.

———

The Therapist closed the Moleskine and placed it in front of him, a wry smile on his face. He lined the book up parallel with the edges of his desk. The glow of the lamp gave his pale skin a jaundiced hue.

He looked up at The Girl, who sat across from him, her face equally as pale. Her stomach distended against the too-small shirt she wore. He gestured to the book. "You should get this back before he notices."

The Girl reached across the desk to take the Moleskine.

"I've made some minor alterations," The Therapist said. "Subliminal things. I doubt he'll notice."

The Girl nodded, shifted in her chair, nervous.

"Things are going well?"

"Yes."

"How are you adjusting to life in Second Tier?"

"It's... different."

"It's been a long time since I've been there myself. Obviously there are a lot of former patients it would be better I didn't run into."

"But it's so big."

"Not as big as you think."

"What about..." She looked down to her stomach.

"How far along are you?"

"Twenty-eight weeks."

"There's still time. In exactly ten more weeks we'll induce. You'll tell him you went into labor while he was at Work, which will be true, and there wasn't time to send word. You'll tell him the child was stillborn."

"What does stillborn mean?"

"It means born dead."

"Oh." Just the thought of it disturbed her. "Will I be able to visit?"

"It'd be better if you didn't. We will place the child with an appropriate Parental Unit. Maybe even your own. It will be well cared for."

The Girl could only nod in response. She stared at the cracked linoleum floor, trying not to cry.

"See The Doctor for some supplements before you head back to Second Tier."

The Girl got up to go, paused at the door. "He talks about leaving The City a lot," she said.

The Therapist brightened, seemed almost proud. "Good. That's... good."

"What's out there?"

For the first time, The Therapist looked unsure of himself. "I don't know. I've never traveled beyond Second Tier. If you're lucky, maybe you'll get the chance."

They stood there in silence, and then The Girl turned and exited the room, hand on her stomach. She walked down The Corridor, thinking about how fortunate she was to have this opportunity, tears rolling down her cheeks.

AFT LAVATORY OCCUPIED

I.

The plane lurched and the man in seat 24A started awake, heart in his throat and stomach where his heart should be. The shifting organs yanked his intestines taut, causing his asshole to clench into a fist. Empty liquor bottles on the tray in front of him spun out of control, like he imagined the plane must be, almost taking out a half-drank cup of coffee. He gripped the armrests—had been the whole time —and dug his fingernails into their soft fabric.

Then as soon as it had begun, the moment of terror ended. Collective adrenaline surged, prompting a smattering of nervous laughter. The captain came on over the loud-speaker to reassure the passengers with his strong voice. A child howled from everywhere at once.

"You can let go of my arm now."

24A looked down to where his right hand clasped not an armrest, but a hairy wrist. He followed the arm up to the smiling man seated next to him. The man's teeth hurt his eyes. He wished for a pair of sunglasses.

"Sorry," he said, releasing his grip. Crescent moon indentations turned pink as blood returned to flesh. "I don't like to fly."

He looked over his shoulder towards the back of the plane, then all the way up to business class. The cabin looked straight out of a cheap movie set. It didn't feel real. He leaned back in his seat and closed his eyes. If he hurried, he could still catch the tail end of that dream. The one that didn't take place on a 400 ton death tube hurtling through the sky.

"Business or pleasure?" his neighbor asked.

So much for that. He gave his neighbor the once over, not bothering to be subtle about it. Thinning hair tied into a ponytail, Hawaiian shirt opened at the top, khaki shorts, open-toe leather sandals—24A needed no further information to form an opinion of the man. He turned away, hoping the guy would take the hint.

"I'm guessing pleasure, otherwise you'd probably be in business class."

24A groaned.

"Oh, I hear ya. We should all be so lucky. I'm on business myself, but as it's personal business, I could only afford to sit in the cheap seats."

The man nudged him in the ribs, prompting 24A's eyes to widen in disbelief.

"Sorry. Full tank? As soon as the captain turns off the fasten seatbelt sign there'll be a mad rush for the restroom, guaranteed. A little turbulence makes for an anxious bladder."

"I'm fine."

"Sure, sure," the man said. "Although, if I may be so bold, your beverages of choice aren't doing much to keep you hydrated. Gotta stay hydrated when you travel."

24A tried to ignore him. But now that the guy had mentioned it, his head hurt like shit. In fact, his whole body ached, like he'd woken up at the bottom of a dog pile. And goddammit if he didn't have to take a piss.

He looked to the back of the plane again. The little figures on the rear-bulkhead glowed red, signifying the toilets were occupied—turbulence be damned. He checked his watch. He had no idea how long he'd slept or how much time remained in the flight. In fact, he realized he didn't even know his final destination. He remembered getting on the plane in... Well, he remembered getting on the plane. Or at least he thought he did.

A quick inventory of his pockets produced 68 cents and a pack of mints. He dropped these in his lap and inspected the seat pocket in front of him. There, between the vomit bag and the in-flight magazine, he found his boarding pass. Tampa? Why the hell would he go there? Certainly not for pleasure. If you asked him, Florida was hell on earth. At least now he knew the date. November 12th.

The man next to him seemed amused by his predicament.

"You don't need it to deplane, you know."

"How's that?"

"Your boarding pass. You don't need it to get off the plane."

What 24A needed was to get away from Ponytail Guy, and fast. So he stood up without another word and got in line for the restroom. If Florida was hell on earth, airline bathrooms functioned as gateways to the real thing. Tiny pockets of punishment to remind you of what awaited the damned in the afterlife.

He ordered water and a cocktail from a passing stewardess, who did a poor job of hiding a sneer. Shit. Did you say stewardess or flight attendant? He'd forgotten which one didn't piss people off. "24A," he told her. He wanted those drinks waiting for him when he got out.

Assuming he ever got in. The person in front of him continued to take their sweet, mile-high time. Maybe they'd gotten lost in the underworld, or had decided not to bother coming back. 24A imagined himself still standing outside the restroom door as the plane began its descent. He imagined himself refusing to give up his spot as a terrorist threatened to blow up the plane. He imagined himself waiting patiently as the plane crashed into the side of a mountain, experiencing the ecstasy of relief as his bladder let loose moments before his death.

That last one made him chuckle. He dug in his heels as a piss-shiver shot through his body. He could wait. He was in no hurry to get back to his seat, let alone his final destination and whatever mystery awaited him there. It was probably the reason he'd tied one on in the first place. Other than the fact he liked to drink. He'd miss this little protective bubble of amnesia once his memory finally returned. He always did.

2.

The plane lurched and the man in seat 24A started awake, testicles bouncing off the bottom of his diaphragm. Empty liquor bottles on the tray in front of him scattered and dropped to the ground, like he imagined the plane must be. His right arm shot out, involuntarily, slamming the man sitting next to him in the chest.

Then as soon as it had begun, the moment of terror ended. Nervous laughter filled the cabin. The captain came on over the loudspeaker to reassure the passengers in a soothing monotone. Thankfully, as evidenced by the lack of wailing, there were no children on the flight.

"That's a mean right you've got there," said the man next to 24A, mock-rubbing his chest.

"Sorry." 24A clenched and unclenched the offending hand. "I don't like to fly."

"You're a lover, not a flyer. I get it."

24A didn't. He looked over his shoulder towards the back of the plane, then all the way up to business class. Was it just the adrenaline or had the cabin gotten smaller? He leaned back in his seat and closed his eyes. Hopefully this little near-death experience hadn't triggered some sort of latent claustrophobia. He had plenty of other issues.

"Me, I'm a lover and a flyer," his neighbor went on.

24A opened his eyes, gave his neighbor a none-too-subtle once over. Sports jersey, baseball cap, sweat pants. He was surprised the guy's first instinct hadn't been to punch him back.

"Nothing breaks the ice like a little turbulence. I met my wife on a particularly bumpy flight out of Toronto. That's also how I met the woman I left her for."

The man flashed a conspiratorial grin, like an unspoken attempt at a high-five. 24A left him hanging.

"You don't say."

His eyes wandered to the back of the plane again, head and bladder throbbing. The miniature couple on the bathroom sign—he'd always assumed they were married—glowed an angry red. He glanced at his watch. How long had he slept? He vaguely remembered taking a piss before takeoff, but that could have been hours ago. Hell, it could have been another flight. Now that he thought about it, he realized he didn't know his final destination.

He rummaged around in his jacket pockets, producing 89 cents and a pack of gum. He dropped these in his lap and inspected the seat pocket in front of him. There, between the food-for-purchase menu and the illustrated safety instructions, he found his boarding pass. Flight 847 to Louisville. May 22nd. What the fuck was in Louisville? A girlfriend? Ex-wife? He thought of the couple on the bathroom sign, pictured them going through a nasty divorce. Cherchez la femme, right? The guy sitting next to him would agree.

Not that 24A planned on giving him the chance. He decided to get up and wait in line for the bathroom instead. There was a special place in hell for people who made small talk with strangers on a plane.

A pregnant woman got in line behind him as he settled in to wait. He tried to avoid eye contact but she locked on like a tractor beam. He forced a smile, like a civilized human, and asked her if she'd like to go in front of him. Of course she said yes.

A piss-shiver shot through his body as he let her squeeze by. Might as well order another drink, he thought. He looked up to the business class bathrooms, which, according to their happily-married green couple, remained unoccupied. 24A cursed their happiness, and cursed his station in life. That exact station eluded him at the moment, but how good could things be for an alcoholic flying coach to Kentucky? He needed to get another drink in him before he remembered. Whatever his problems, another drink usually solved them.

3.

The plane lurched and the man in seat 24A started awake, tongue thick in his throat. His muscles tensed, causing the flimsy plastic cup in his hand to crack. The watered-down dregs of a Jack and Coke splashed the seat tray in front of him.

Nervous laughter filled the cabin, laughter that felt directed at him. The captain came on over the loudspeaker to reassure the passengers with a disc jockey delivery. In a miraculous turn of events, the infant in the seat across the aisle hadn't stirred.

"Now that's what I call sleeping like a baby," the man seated next to him said.

24A put up his seat tray and wiped a sticky hand on his pants.

"Must be nice. I fucking hate flying."

He looked down the aisle for the—stewardess? —Flight attendant? His head pounded. He needed another drink.

"It could be worse," his neighbor said.

24A turned to the man, gave him an aggressive once over. Designer glasses, close-cropped power donut, business casual. Surely the guy could take a hint, right?

Wrong.

"My last flight," the man went on, "the guy next to me stormed the cockpit. Told the air marshall I had talked him into it. Took me three hours to convince the TSA otherwise."

"Uh huh."

"For the record, I'm in no way suggesting you do the same. In fact, I have an affidavit I'd like you to sign absolving me of any guilt should you decide to wig out."

The guy reached for his briefcase. 24A instinctively put his hand inside his jacket. His fingers closed around nothing, but the guy next to him didn't know that.

"Take it easy, buddy, it was just a joke." The man moved away from the briefcase.

Why had 24A done that? He looked to the back of the plane, head and bladder throbbing in unison. The little people on the bathroom sign glowed red, like lives on a death toll infographic. He glanced at his watch. How long had he slept? Better yet, where the fuck was he going? He remembered hustling to catch a connecting flight. Or at least he thought he did.

A surge of panic filled his chest like a dying breath. He rummaged around in the rest of his pockets, then inspected the seat back in front of him. There, behind the Sky Mall magazine, he found his boarding pass. He checked the date and flight number while the guy next to him made a show of looking out the window and ignoring him. The December 16th flight to—Milwaukee? What business did he have in that tire fire? He stood up and opened his jacket for the guy next to him to see. "Just a joke," he said, then headed for the restroom.

As soon as he'd taken his place in line, a pregnant woman materialized behind him. If not in a previous life, he must have done something on a previous flight to deserve this. They forced smiles and ignored each other, like civilized human beings. No way was he going to let her get in front of him. He'd have to storm the business class bathrooms or wet his pants.

A piss-shiver shot through his body and ran up his arm, causing a reflexive knock.

"Cool your jets, buddy, I'm pinching one off."

He shared a look of resignation with the pregnant woman.

"God I need a drink."

He'd thought it, but the words had come out of her mouth.

"It's on me." He flagged down the flight attendant and ordered a round. Figured it would tip his karma in the other direction. The flight attendant didn't blink twice at the pregnant woman's request for booze.

24A looked towards the business class restrooms. According to their little green people they remained unoccupied. He calculated the odds of an uptight airline employee intercepting him if he made a break for it. God, he hated flying. Some life changes were definitely in order. But first he needed that drink.

4.

The plane lurched and the man in seat 24A started awake. His hand shot out, knocking a half-drank Jack and Coke all over the leg of the guy sitting next to him.

"Shit."

Awkwardness supplanted fear as he scrambled for napkins. He looked up and the—stewardess? Flight attendant?—appeared out of nowhere with a handful, like a guardian angel of paper goods.

"Thanks," he said as he sheepishly took the stack and handed it to the guy. "I think this would be less embarrassing if you took over from here."

"For who?" his neighbor replied, in better humor than expected. He was an older gentleman, one you could describe as grandfatherly or non-threatening. But as pleasant as he appeared, 24A had no desire to engage him in conversation. He forced a polite smile.

"Fly much?" the man said as he dabbed away at his crotch.

"Feels like my whole life's been one gigantic plane ride."

24A looked over his shoulder towards the rear of the plane. All the excitement had brought along with it an intense need to urinate.

"It could be worse," his neighbor said.

But 24A had already vacated his seat. He walked to the back of the plane, head and bladder throbbing. The little people on the restroom bulkhead glowed red. He glanced at his watch. He had no idea how long he'd slept or how much time remained in the flight. In fact, he realized he didn't even know his final destination. Or the date. Try as he might, he didn't even remember getting on the plane. He remembered getting a drink at the airport bar beforehand, but he always had a drink beforehand. A few, actually.

He stuck his hands in his jacket pockets, came up with a ball of lint and a crumpled boarding pass. He smoothed out the paper and checked the flight information. Atlanta? In July? Why would he be going there? Nothing but strippers and thugs in that burg.

Instinctively his hand went inside his jacket. He felt the smooth contours of hard plastic. Was he carrying? He wasn't about to check on a plane full of people. A piss-shiver shot through his body. He gave the bathroom door an impatient knock.

"Cool your jets, buddy, I'm talking to my accountant."

He looked up to the business class restrooms, which according to their sign remained unoccupied. He calculated the odds of a flight attendant intercepting him if he made a break for it.

That's when he noticed a familiar face up in business class. Designer glasses, close-cropped power donut, business casual. He didn't know where from, but he knew he knew the guy. As an acquaintance of a business class passenger, he should be allowed access to the business class lavatory, right?

He started towards the forward cabin of the plane, not realizing he still had his hand thrust inside his jacket. A few concerned looks turned to collective unease. From there it was a hop, skip and a jump to somebody shouting, "He's got a gun!"

24A ignored the ensuing panic, laser-focused on the familiar man. By now all of business class had turned in their seats to assess the situation, the familiar man included. His eyes went wide as he saw 24A bearing down on him, hand inside his jacket like Napoleon Bonaparte.

"He's headed for the cockpit!" someone yelled.

That's when the hero in the sports jersey stuck out a sweatpanted leg. 24A saw stars as he landed nose first, heard the crunch and felt the accompanying rush of blood. I could really use another drink, he thought, as half of premium economy piled on top of him and his vision became a pinhole in a field of black.

5.

The plane lurched and the man in seat 24A started awake, heart in his throat and stomach where his heart should be. The shifting organs yanked his intestines taut, causing his asshole to clench into a fist. Empty liquor bottles on the tray in front of him spun out of control, like he imagined the plane must be. He gripped the armrests—had been the whole time—and dug his fingernails into their soft fabric.

Then as soon as it had begun, the moment of terror ended. Collective adrenaline surged, prompting a smattering of nervous laughter. The captain came on over the loud-speaker to reassure the passengers with his strong voice. A child howled from everywhere at once.

"You can let go of my arm now."

24A looked down to where his right hand clasped a hairy wrist. He followed the arm up to the smiling man seated next to him. He knew the man's face before he saw it, but he didn't know the man's identity.

"Sorry," he said, releasing his grip. "I don't like to fly."

He looked over his shoulder towards the back of the plane, then all the way up to business class. The cabin looked straight out of a cheap movie set. He leaned back in his seat and closed his eyes. If he hurried, he could still catch the tail end of that dream. The one that ended with his feet on solid ground.

"Business or pleasure?" his neighbor asked.

So much for that. He gave his neighbor the once over, for his benefit, not bothering to be subtle about it. He already knew what he would find: thinning hair tied into a ponytail, Hawaiian shirt opened at the top, khaki shorts, open-toe leather sandals. He turned away, hoping the other man would take the hint.

"I'm guessing pleasure, otherwise you'd probably be in business class."

24A groaned.

"Oh, I hear ya. We should all be so lucky. I'm on business myself, but as it's personal business, I could only afford to sit in the cheap seats."

The man nudged him in the ribs, prompting 24A's eyes to open wide in disbelief.

"Sorry. Full tank? As soon as the Captain turns off the seatbelt sign there'll be a mad rush for the bathroom, guaranteed. A little turbulence makes for an anxious bladder."

"I'm fine."

But now that the guy had mentioned it, goddammit if he didn't have to piss.

He looked to the back of the plane. The little figures on the rear-bulkhead glowed red, signifying the toilets were occupied—turbulence be damned. He checked his watch. He had no idea how long he'd slept or how much time remained in the flight. In fact, he realized he didn't even know his final destination. Or the date. He remembered getting on the plane. Or at least he thought he did.

A quick inventory of his pockets produced 62 cents and a pack of mints. Inside his jacket he found a heavy duty vape pen made of molded plastic. He smoked? The sudden urge for nicotine answered his question.

He dropped the items in his lap and inspected the seat pocket in front of him. There, between the vomit bag and the in-flight magazine, he found his boarding pass. A November 12th flight to—Tampa? He didn't know what awaited him there, but he vaguely remembered an equally unpleasant trip to said city in his recent past. In his humble opinion, Florida was hell on Earth. The man next to him seemed amused by his predicament.

"Looks like someone forgot their Nicorette."

24A needed to get away from Ponytail guy, and fast. So he stood up without another word and got in line for the restroom. If Florida was hell on earth, airline bathrooms functioned as gateways to the real thing. Tiny pockets of punishment to remind you of what awaited the damned in the afterlife.

He ordered water and a cocktail from a passing flight attendant, who did a poor job of hiding a sneer. "24A," he told her. He wanted those drinks waiting for him when he got out.

Assuming he ever got in. The person in front of him continued to take their sweet, mile-high time. Maybe they'd gotten lost in the underworld, or had decided not to bother coming back. He imagined himself still standing outside the restroom door as the plane crashed into the side of a mountain, experiencing the ecstasy of relief as his bladder let loose moments before his death. A piss-shiver shot through his body and ran up his arm, causing a reflexive knock.

As if on cue, the door folded open to reveal a pair of angry eyes. Below them, a fist clutched a paper towel to a bloody nose.

"You okay?"

A familiar voice answered him, one he couldn't quite place. Something about it rubbed him the wrong way. Like when you hear your own recorded voice played back to you.

"Fucking turbulence," the man said as he pushed past him.

24A didn't waste any time—he locked himself inside the bathroom and decided not to emerge until the plane landed. Meanwhile, the man with the bloody nose took his seat. His seat. 24A.

"What the hell happened to you?" the man in the Hawaiian shirt asked the man with the bloody nose. The man with the bloody nose just glared. Then he hit the flight attendant call button and proceeded to rummage around in the seat pocket in front of him.

6.

The plane lurched and the man in seat 24A started awake. It would be a couple minutes before he realized he'd wet himself, at which point he would shut his eyes and go back to sleep.

THE GOSPEL OF X

Chapter 1

1. These are the words of the Prophet writ flesh, transcribed by His servant in the days following the ascension. May they serve as the cornerstone of His church, that the blind might hear and the deaf might see.

2. For it is not unto Him to return sight He hath not taken, nor to restore hearing that hath been lost. Instead let the blind rejoice at the sound of His voice, and let the deaf look upon His face, that they might prove their devotion unto Him.

3. And if He hath plucked out thine eye, covet it not. If He hath severed thine ear, turn thy head. For only by His pleasure is atonement achieved, and only by pain can we atone, that servant and master might be joined again on the plane dividing our worlds.

4. For He was born not of a woman but of the firmament, one star scattered amongst many. And His light did shine brighter than that of His siblings, and they became jealous and did conspire against Him.

5. Thus they went before their father and said unto him, In His pride He thinketh himself more powerful than thee.

6. And this did anger their father, so he extinguished his son's light and cast Him from the heavens. And the Prophet descended unto Earth, taking on human form that He might experience humankind.

7. For though the years of man are short, He is everlasting, and hath watched us tear down that which we have built time and again.

8. And lo, the Prophet emerged naked from the wilderness, pale skin indifferent to the sun. His hairless body exhibited not the physical manifestations of human sex, and His eyes were points of red.

9. There came He upon His servant drawing water at a well, and I did tremble before Him, saying, Whither camest Thou? Art Thou man or woman? God or devil?

10. And saying nothing, He laid His hands upon me, and lo, a peace washed over me. He then raised me to my feet and looked within my heart and in that moment I knew Him.

11. Then gave I the Prophet drink, for in knowing Him His thirst became my own. And I lifted Him up and carried Him to my home, where I prepared a place for Him in my own chamber.

12. It was there that I tended unto His recovery, supplementing His strength with mine. But the body of man is imperfect, so I offered unto Him my daughter, that through her He might be made whole.

13. And although she objected, the girl obeyed and gave herself unto Him, and afterwards she marveled at the things which He did show her.

14. And I became afraid, because He had placed his mark upon her, and she was not yet given unto marriage.

15. So I thought to conceal her from the other members of the village, for fear they would seek out the one that had done this unto her, and coming upon the Prophet, would not understand that He was not of this place, neither man nor woman.

16. And He opened His mouth as if to answer my unspoken thoughts. No words came forth yet I heard Him still.

17. **Which of these is the head of the house**, I heard Him say. **The man or the woman? Hast thou not proven this by giving unto me thy daughter?**

18. And He bade me worry not, and invited me to lie between Him and the girl that we might rest.

19. And we gave of ourselves unto Him, even unto sleep, where we continued our communion amongst stranger worlds.

20. And when I awoke the next morning the Prophet had gone. My daughter in her sleep had heard Him not, so I clothed myself and went out unto the day.

21. And I came upon Him in the village center conversing amongst the elders. I knew it was He though His appearance had changed. The soft features of His face had thinned and hardened, His body had grown in size and strength. White hairs adorned His chest, and trailed beneath the robe He wore. I followed it downward, wondering if the ambiguous nature of His sex had also changed.

22. Why hidest thou our learned guest?, The elders said. For though He is foreign, He converses most eloquently.

23. And it surprised me to find it so. Since the communion of our spirits He had mastered the language of the land. And despite His transformation He exuded a feminine air which He did wield over the men.

24. And they began to quarrel over which of them would host our guest next, but the Prophet declined, choosing instead to stay with the one that had found Him.

25. This caused much consternation amongst the elders, as I was not a person of high standing within our village.

26. And as they grumbled still the Prophet took up a stone and threw it into a nearby pack of dogs. The mongrels scattered and regrouped, their numbers lessened. Another stone was thrown and the result was the same. Soon there was only one. It had been struck by a rock and blood issued from its head, yet still it waited.

27. **It is the servant that chooseth the master**, the Prophet said, **Though the master thinks he chooseth the servant**.

28. And I felt honor at His words, though I did not fully comprehend their meaning at the time.

Chapter 2

1. The next day the Prophet accompanied me thence to forage for food. And lo, we came upon two brothers tending their father's flock. And when He bid them good morning the brothers mocked Him, saying, Go up, bald head. Go up, pink eye.

2. This angered the Prophet, and He relieved the elder child

of his staff and struck them both until they could no longer walk.

3. And I became afraid, for their father was a man of wealth and power within our village.

4. But the Prophet said, **Be not afraid. For not only hath they paid for their disrespect, they shall provide us our meat**, and He set them as bait for larger prey.

5. The whole while they cried out for mercy, but the Prophet answered them not, and soon they were devoured. Then we fell upon those that devoured them.

6. And we returned to the village triumphant, the bringers of meat, and slayers of the beast that did kill the two children, and their family did honor us.

7. My sons are gone, The father said, But verily our flock has been preserved.

8. Then they called upon the villagers, saying, Come, let us celebrate. And they did eat and drink to excess. And I begged the Prophet to forgive me my doubt, and in His grace, He showed forgiveness.

9. And that night the Prophet took unto Him the daughter of one of the elders. And He bid me join them as reward for my loyalty, and I did accept.

10. And the next day the elder came to the Prophet, worried that his daughter had not returned home. And the Prophet said, **Fear not, for she keepeth company with me.**

11. This angered the elder, and seeing that she kept company with me as well, he admonished the Prophet, saying, Thou didst not ask a father's permission. She is a child, betrothed to another, and was not yours to take.

12. The Prophet sought to calm the man, saying, **Does the ground giveth permission for the rain to fall? Does the sun giveth permission for the flower to bloom? Nay, both are the product of nature, and nature needeth not permission from itself.**

13. And the elder, his mind clouded by the Prophet's reasoning, replied, But what of the dowry bought with my daughter's virtue? Whence shall come the payment I am owed by right for the child?

14. And the Prophet said, **Virtue is not easily divined. Go ye and claim payment still.**

15. Thus the Prophet released the girl unto her father, both men having been appeased.

Chapter 3

1. And lo, the Prophet was summoned unto the wilderness by His siblings, with a message from their father.

2. And His siblings said unto Him, Our father is ready to celebrate thy return, but only if thou hast humbled thine heart.

3. And the Prophet was sorely tempted, for He yearned for the companionship of His kin, but He relented not, for He would not submit unto his father's will.

4. Father knowest thy desires, His siblings said unto Him. These creatures are not yours to rule.

5. And still, the Prophet refused.

6. Very well, the siblings said. Our father giveth unto thee a

year's time, after which thou shalt be retrieved. Thou mayest live amongst them, but sow not the ground with thine own seed, for it is an abomination in our father's eyes.

7. And the Prophet, in His wisdom, agreed, but in His heart meant it not.

8. And that very day, two men came seeking the Prophet's counsel. They each sought to adopt the same child into their household. Since the boy was an orphan and had no kin, they brought the matter before the Prophet to mediate.

9. **Brothers,** He said. **Why do ye quarrel over this boy?** And they answered Him and said, We only want to provide for the child.

10. Then the Prophet turned to the boy and said, **Which of these men would thou go with? Both command wealth and power, and either would make a fine father.**

11. And the boy replied, Neither, my Lord, for it is the desire of both men to lie with me.

12. And at this the Prophet did laugh, and He said unto them, **Since ye cannot agree amongst yourselves, neither will the boy decide, I shall take him for my own. When I am done ye may do with him as ye will.**

13. And though none were happy with the Prophet's decision, they obeyed. Such had the Prophet's status grown within the village.

14. And when He had tired of the the boy, the Prophet sent him away, saying, **Your days of service are done. Go and serve well another master.**

15. And the boy begged the Prophet to keep him still, despite having witnessed the depravity of His desire.

16. But the Prophet would have nothing further to do with the child, and turned him unto the street. And neither nobleman did take him, for his appearance had been marked and his virtue spent.

Chapter 4

1. Word of the Prophet's wisdom spread to nearby villages, and the people did come. And He went out unto them and taught them, saying:

2. **Do what ye will and explore the furthest reaches of experience, for there is pleasure to be found.**

3. **Concern yourself not with the father's rejection of the flesh, for the father is not the man. Only once ye have satisfied yourself can ye fulfill the desire of others.**

4. **The body is a temple where reverence must be shown. If a man enters therein he shall do as instructed. The priests instruct only to serve those who worship.**

5. **For the servant thinks they are the master of their desire, but it is the desire of the master that they must know.**

6. **Therefore seek ye the path of imperfection, for perfection in others can only be achieved through the degradation of self.**

7. **For lust is not patient or kind. The tyranny of its**

demands are militant in nature. It is like unto a strong wind. Once a door hath been opened, though that door may again be shut, the wind hath already entered therein.

8. **And although quickly forgotten, that wind is become the room, indistinguishable from the rest, fallen candles and scattered parchment the only witness to its presence.**

9. **And when He had finished they implored Him, saying, Thou hast fed our souls, now feedeth thee our stomachs, for they are empty and we have traveled far.**

10. And He went unto the river and placed His hand upon the surface and the fish did rise. But the crowd was too slow in reaching for them and the current bore them downstream.

11. And He said unto them, **Hurry, follow the river that ye may gather the fish before they are swept away**, but the crowd refused.

12. It is too hot, they said, And our feet are tired. Canst thou not summon the fish yet again? And the Prophet became angered by their laziness.

13. Then came before Him a small child, urged by its parents to beg for food. And the Prophet instructed it to wade within the river. And lo, the wind rose up and the child was washed away.

14. And the child's mother cried out to the Prophet, Save our child, lest it drown.

15. And the Prophet answered her saying, **It is too hot, and**

**I am tired. Ye shall find the child downstream with
the fish.**

16. And the mother cursed the Prophet, and rent her clothes
and did weep openly. Only then did the Prophet console her,
drawing her nakedness unto him. And the husband showed
them his back but yea, the crowd did watch.

Chapter 5

1. And when the needs of the village became too great, the
Prophet instructed His servant to seek out and anoint
priests, that they might carry out His work.

2. **They must be strong of body and soft of will,** He
said, **that I might mold them in my image.**

3. And lo, I searched the lands, and returned with three
young men to present unto Him. And He took them in that
He might test them body and spirit, and they did pass.

4. Then gave He unto them the trappings of the priesthood,
firstly shaving the hair from their bodies, in the image of
when He first appeared.

5. Then painted He their eyes black with soot, saying unto
them, **Though they appear close from a great
distance, each star is a single light within the vast
darkness.**

6. Then laced He strips of hide through the flesh of their
forearms, the long ends barbed with stone and glass. He
then tended unto their wounds, saying, **The hand that
chastiseth must also caress.**

7. Then traced He a ring about their heads with a sharp

stone, that their faces might be streaked in blood as a sign of their station. And He instructed them to reopen the wounds daily, that the scar might thicken to form a crown.

8. Then relieved He them of their sex, in the image of when He first appeared. He then cauterized the wounds with fire, but soon after the boys became feverish and died.

9. Their deaths weighed heavy on the Prophet's mind. He retreated unto Himself, preserving the boys' sex in jars of wine that He might reflect upon them. He became drunk off the wine and refused to eat, and His followers in the village did worry.

10. But after seven days He emerged, and went out unto the wilderness to commune with His siblings.

11. And lo, He returned with two who were of like mind, outcasts like Himself, and they became His priests. They received the modifications to their bodies and their wounds did heal.

12. Their sex was neither masculine nor feminine, and He clothed them not, for their appearance struck fear into the hearts of certain men and desire into others. And those who feared became enemies of the Prophet, while those who desired the priests became His disciples.

13. And they did submit themselves unto the will of the priests in the name of the Prophet, and life in the village continued in this way.

Chapter 6

1. It was at this time the store of my wealth did dwindle, and I went before the Prophet and fell to my knees, saying,

Forgive me, for I have failed thee. I can no longer shelter thee and thine Priests, for I am a man of simple means and my possessions are few.

2. And He lifted me to my feet and said, **Rise up, my servant. Thou hast already given all. There are many who still have much to give.** And He went out unto the village and instructed them to raise a temple for He and His Priests to reside in.

3. It was built in the image of the great temples of the past, which spread not across the land but towards the sky, and at the top was constructed a holy chamber where none but the Prophet and His priests might enter.

4. And though its stature did not hold measure to those structures, the sight of it did fill His servants with wonder.

5. Contained within were pools for bathing and a vast cellar wherein wine was kept. Included also were many chambers for public and private pleasure. The door required no key for young supplicants to enter, and only the Prophet's permission for them to leave.

6. There did He commune with His brothers in holy ritual atop the temple, the night sky lighting up as if the sun had refused to set.

7. And as reward for my service He did entrust me with the overseeing of His household. And He placed His priests in my charge to collect tribute from those who might resist their duty.

8. And there were murmurs against the Prophet amongst the richest men of the village. For it is easier for the poor to forsake what little they have, than for the wealthy to sacrifice even a portion of their riches.

9. But the Prophet said, **Worry thyself not. It is they that hath built this place, and its door is open unto them.**

Chapter 7

1. Now in those days the great empires of man had fallen, their powers scattered to the corners of the land. But progress moveth ever forward, and lo, a group of men banded together under the banner of like notions of god and government, and began exerting their influence.

2. And smaller groups that had been fruitful in peace were powerless against the will of these men, and so bent or were broken.

3. And the servants of this god declared, There can only be one that all must worship. We shall spread his word, thereby increasing his heavenly kingdom.

4. And the rulers saw wisdom in this for their own purpose, so forbade not the acolytes from spreading this agenda. And under their sword many lesser nations fell.

5. But the Prophet and His village remained on the outskirts of the land, and were considered neither a threat nor an asset.

6. Still, outsiders made the pilgrimage to partake of His teachings, and word was brought back to those who worshipped the foreign god and they did harbor ill will in their hearts.

7. One such pilgrim was a pious man's daughter, who forsook her god and family to enter the discipleship of the Prophet.

8. But the girl lacked dedication, and over time grew complacent. Not wishing to fulfill her duties unto the Prophet and His priests, she took her leave to seek enlightenment elsewhere.

9. But one day she returned, and came unto the Prophet and said, I am with child. Relieve me of this burden, for I am not ready.

10. And the Prophet welcomed her back into His temple and rendered her unto the care of His priests. And lo, she did emerge free of child, but from that day her womb refused to bring forth fruit.

11. And the girl returned unto her father, who went before the rulers of the land and demanded the honor of his daughter be avenged, and the rulers asked, What would thou have us do? And the Pious Man said, I would have the Prophet dead.

12. And the rulers agreed, for it was the servants of their god who kept the populace in line. So they gave unto him a horse and some men and said, Do what thou wilt.

Chapter 8

1. And as the Prophet's influence spread across the land, so too did the grumblings of the wealthy.

2. Seeing this, the Prophet threw a great feast in their honor. And after He raised his cup unto their health, He retired to His temple to get drunk with His priests.

3. And the villagers did eat and drink to excess, but the hearts of the rich softened not.

4. Why does He not join us? they said. Does He think to appease us with drink that we might forget?

5. And lo, it was during this revelry that the Pious Man and his escort arrived at the village.

6. Where is the one they call the Prophet?, the Pious Man said, That He may answer for the crimes He hath committed.

7. And I stood before them and said, What hath thou accused Him of?

8. And the Pious Man signalled to his escort and they did attack the celebration.

9. And the rich men saw their chance to be rid of the Prophet, and in their cowardice led the escort to the temple door. Come forth! They called unto the Prophet. For there are men here that would speak with thee.

10. And the Prophet emerged, accompanied by a woman who hid not her nakedness, and both were drunk on wine.

11. **Who disturbeth our celebration?** demanded the Prophet. And the Pious Man stepped forth and struck Him across the face.

12. And the Prophet called upon His priests, but they responded not for they slept under the influence of drink.

13. And the escort stripped the Prophet of His clothes and dragged Him through the village to the top of a hill. There they forced Him to His knees and bound Him to the trunk of a tree with His arms bent behind Him.

14. And the elders who had once fought for His favor denounced Him and spit upon Him.

15. And the Prophet laughed and said unto them, **A servant
who thinketh himself the master does not know
whom he truly serves.**

16. This angered the elders all the more and they began to
pelt Him with stones. And the Pious Man intervened,
saying, His death shall not be quick.

17. Then the Pious Man cleaned His wounds with vinegar
and did mock Him, saying, Didst thou not say it was by pain
we must atone?

18. And the Prophet did fix his gaze upon the man, and
spoke without words, saying, **Yea, but it is only by my
pleasure that atonement may be achieved.**

19. And in that moment the Pious Man knew the Prophet
and it did frighten him, for he felt the power of His
appetite. Then took he his knife and with the last of his
strength put out the Prophet's eyes, that He might no
longer speak in such a manner.

20. And the Prophet laughed and screamed at the loss of
His sight, as the dogs howl at the night.

21. And in my weakness I said unto Him, Call out unto thine
father, that he might rescue thee, but He would not.

Chapter 9

1. And the next morning after they had slept off their drink,
the Prophet's siblings did attempt to free Him. But the
escort of the Pious Man numbered too many and did beat
them back.

2. So shed they their human skin to destroy the escort, but

lo, seven siblings loyal unto their father appeared wielding swords of light and did slay them. Then stood they vigil to ensure the Prophet's demise.

3. And the Pious Man did prepare a great meal to break his fast, and set his table under the tree to which the Prophet was bound. And though He had not sight, the Prophet salivated at the smell.

4. And I yearned to help the Prophet, even unto my own death, but in the weakness of my fear I did not, and was ashamed.

5. And the Pious Man continued to torment the Prophet that day. And as the Prophet weakened, so too did His appearance, reverting to its original state, neither male nor female.

6. And the Pious Man's escort did study the Prophet, and sparing not His pain gained intimate knowledge of His sex.

7. And the Prophet said unto them, **Thinketh thou to destroy me by that which giveth me life? Ye are here by my will and in your selfishness ye fulfill my purpose.**

8. And when his life had dwindled to a flicker, the Prophet spoke, saying, **My Father appears before me on a great chariot of light pulled by the eight masters of the sky. He is here to escort me unto the firmament from whence I came.**

9. **And he hath brought seven maidens to soothe me, and seven mothers to feed me, and seven crones to bathe me.**

10. **But fear not, for I shall return to take back my temple, and those who reside within its halls shall be**

slain, and those who live within its shadow shall see mercy.

11. And I shall set up my kingdom on this world. And the souls of those who have gone before shall fall from the sky and fertilize the ground in which their bodies are laid, and they shall rise up from the grave to be with me again.

12. And I looked but saw not these things.

13. And the Pious Man cut out the Prophet's tongue and fed it to the dogs. And lo, the mongrel that didst swallow the meat bore a familiar scar upon its head.

Chapter 10

1. On the the third day of His suffering the Prophet gave up His spirit and died.

2. The seven siblings, having witnessed His death, returned to the firmament to inform their father, taking with them the bodies of the priests they had slain. The Prophet's body they did not take.

3. And I rent my clothes and cursed the sky, saying, What kind of father abandons his son, even unto death?

4. And the Pious Man said, His body is of the earth and belongs not to His father, but to me.

5. Then the Pious Man ordered the Prophet's body committed unto the flames, so that He might not fulfill that which He had prophesied.

6. And though I struggled against the men of the escort to prevent it, I succeeded not.

7. And when the crowd had dispersed and the embers burned low, His servant spirited away His remains and did bury them in the wilderness by the well where they had first met.

8. Afterwards I wandered for many moons, settling in a land far from the reach of the Pious Man and those he served. Its people had no god but the earth and they did welcome me.

9. It was there that I began transcribing The Prophet's words upon my own flesh with a needle and dye, as was the tradition taught by those people.

10. And I partook of the root of transcendence, as was also their tradition, and did experience a powerful vision. The Prophet appeared to me as a cloud of light and took me up unto a palace that did move within the sky.

11. And there He revealed unto me His true form, surrounded by the forms of many others I understood not, and yea, I was afraid.

12. And the Prophet spoke unto us in many languages at once, and we heard Him though His mouth moved not.

13. And He said, **Be not afraid, for these priests are your brethren. They are of many worlds, both of the future and the past.**

14. And He showed unto us things which would come to be, on our own worlds and others. Cities of stone and glass, above the clouds and beneath the ocean. Strange lands and stranger people, as well as atonements of indescribable pleasure.

15. And the Prophet said unto us, **Bear this record and be blessed, and blessed be those that receive it.**

16. **For ye are priests and princes amongst men, and servants unto the flesh. The foundation upon which I shall rebuild my temple and the mortar that shall bind its bricks.**

17. **And lo, I say unto you, the day shall come when I return, and together we shall bind our enemies and smite them with the lash.**

18. **And we shall enslave their sons and daughters for their own edification. And those that submit not shall be put to death.**

19. And He revealed unto us the Pious Man, laid out upon a table of stone, his flesh peeled back from his body. And though he had no lips, he did smile.

20. And lo, a trumpet sounded and there appeared a great blinding light. I awoke from my vision and fell to my knees and kissed the earth, for I knew I stood upon consecrated ground.

21. And verily I say unto you, these are the words of the Prophet writ flesh. Let no man add unto them or take away, but let us testify unto all that heareth until the day He returns, bringing with Him our reward.

22. Amen and amen.

NOBODY RIDES FOR FREE

Part One

Rake watched the blacktop melt into the horizon as Trisha hiked up her skirt and stuck out her thumb. Coarse hair sprouted from her dirt-smeared legs, but Rake doubted it would hurt their prospects. Under all the grime Trisha was still a piece of ass. And if they put enough mileage between themselves and the shit that went down in Bellamy, they could splurge for a motel room and clean themselves up.

"Fish on the line," Trisha said as a Dodge A100 crested the hill.

Rake shaded his eyes and turned to look. "Is it slowing?"

"Think so."

Trisha waved at the approaching vehicle. A damp circle formed between her shoulder blades where her tank top pressed against her skin. Rake hocked up a wad of phlegm and spit it onto the asphalt next to her cowboy boots. She shot him a death stare.

"I had a bug in my mouth." The gob of mucus started to sizzle.

"Save your spit." Trisha turned her attention back to the road. "You might need it."

A slideshow of compromising images flashed through Rake's mind, prompting a grimace.

"Do you always have to play with your food before you eat it?"

It was a rhetorical question. She'd been that way since childhood. He, on the other hand, had always dutifully gobbled down anything set in front of him.

"Don't hate the player..." Trisha called over her shoulder.

"Yeah, yeah. This isn't a fucking game. We should probably lay low for a while."

"Just follow my lead."

Rake threw his hands up in exasperation.

"Whatever you say, Sis."

The van's turn signal blinked on and the driver angled toward the side of the road. Trisha shouldered a black dufflebag and approached the passenger door, flashing her million-dollar smile. Purple lipstick stained her teeth. The driver leaned over and pushed the door open.

"That a yes?" Trisha said over the rumble of the engine. The driver was an older man, dressed in a trucker hat, stained white t-shirt, and overalls.

"Window don't roll down."

Rake limped up beside her, his left foot dragging in the gravel. Trisha played the lure, but they made it a point not to hide Rake from view. Drivers didn't appreciate surprises. And as much as he hated it, they could always switch roles on the off chance a twist or a queer picked them up.

"Got room for two?" Trisha said when the man didn't elaborate.

"How far you going?"

Rake peered into the van. The engine housing rested between the driver and passenger seats, an odd feature of the A100's design. Despite the sound insulated cover, the thing made a shit-ton of noise.

"As far as you can take us," Rake said.

"Going pretty far."

"That suits us fine."

The driver grunted, turned his head back toward the road to think on it.

"Alright, then."

Trisha slid the side door open and hopped in. The van sported a single bench seat in back and an open interior. Rake climbed into the passenger seat, taking extra care not to put pressure on his bad foot. He wore mismatched tennis shoes.

"Hurt yourself?" the driver asked.

"Just a sprain."

"Sprains don't bleed."

Rake looked down at the foot.

"Stepped in some roadkill."

The driver grunted a second time. Rake shut the door and checked the sideview. *Objects in mirror are closer than they appear*. As they pulled away he could see the wet spot where he'd hocked his phlegm. By the time the unmarked Crown Victoria shot past it, the loogie had completely evaporated.

The trio rode in silence for a good hour, the hitchers content to be off their feet and out of the sun. Wind from the driver-side window whipped their hair, drying sweat cold against their scalps. A blur of flat, barren land raced by. When they pulled into the truck stop 100 miles later, they both felt a lot better than they looked.

The driver exited the vehicle without a word. As soon as he disappeared from view Trisha leaned forward and jabbed Rake in the arm.

"Ow, what?"

She gestured to the interior of the van, a mischievous spark in her eye.

"This looks like the van from that chainsaw movie."

Rake rolled his eyes. She feigned offense.

"Just making an observation is all."

"The driver ain't the dangerous one in that movie, remember?"

That earned him a flash of purple Chiclets. He liked that she liked when he talked tough.

"You got lipstick on your teeth."

Rake faced front while she dragged a finger across her chompers. He contemplated treating himself to a corn dog. It took a moment for him to see the driver in his periphery, staring at him through the passenger window.

"Jesus!" Rake gripped the dashboard as if bracing for impact.

"Got any money for gas?" the driver said. The glass muffled his voice.

Rake let out a nervous laugh, tried to roll down the window, then remembered it didn't work. "You scared the shit out of me, man."

The driver continued to stare.

"Look, we don't... WE DON'T REALLY HAVE MUCH MONEY." Rake glanced at Trisha and the dufflebag. "BUT I COULD DRIVE A SPELL IF YOU'RE TIRED."

More silence. The driver seemed to look right through him.

"We'll figure it out later."

"Sure. Sure thing."

The driver unnerved him, but Rake shook it off. That's what the revolver was for. Unfortunately it was the only piece of hardware to make it out of Bellamy.

Trisha leaned forward to hiss in Rake's ear. "Looks like the game chose us," she said, giving him a playful bite.

———

Officer Pendleton guided her unmarked police cruiser into the parking lot of the truck stop. The A100 had just pulled back out onto the highway, so she figured she had about five minutes to piss and refuel before she lost them. Hopefully they'd be stopping for the night soon, because she hadn't slept since the standoff and her eyes had started to glaze over. The cacophony of gunfire playing on loop inside her head would only keep her awake for so long.

She'd been placed on administrative leave, which was

standard procedure, but somebody was bound to notice she hadn't returned her vehicle to the carpool. Especially after her blowout with the Chief. On top of that, she had a psych evaluation scheduled the next day. Again, standard procedure, but missing it would be an instant red flag.

She stepped out of the ripeness of the Crown Vic and breathed in diesel. She got a jump on undoing her belt as she made her way towards the restroom, counting off the list of provisions she needed in her mind as she went. *Coffee, air freshener, corndog...*

She got to the bathroom and stuck out her hand, but the door handle refused to turn.

"Shit."

She hoped this wasn't one of those places that made you sign out a key. She didn't have time to track down an attendant. She tried pounding her fist against the door instead.

"Jakes is occupied."

The geezer's voice sounded like death. Ten to one she had a *code deuce* on her hands. Shitting while intoxicated. She pounded some more.

"Open up. Police business."

"I'm glad you're here, Officer." The door unlocked with an audible click. "Cuz this here's a record breaker, and I'm gonna need me a witness."

Pendleton took a step back, hand on her gun. The door remained shut. An invitation had been made, but she reckoned it was up to her to accept it or not. She looked towards the highway. It disappeared in a straight shot, but the van was already out of sight.

Fuck it, she thought. She'd get a cup and piss in the car. She sprinted for the mart, pants still undone, as a chorus of unholy sounds followed behind her.

———

An hour later the temperature had dropped by a good ten degrees. Trisha leaned back with her knees facing opposite directions, skirt riding up around her thighs, enjoying the flow of cool air. The driver hadn't looked in the rearview once. She hated being ignored. Throw some boredom into the mix and you had yourself a steaming batch of trouble.

"We really appreciate you picking us up." Trisha had to hunch and duck walk to the front of the vehicle to be heard over the rumbling Slant 6.

Rake realized her intentions immediately, and chimed in to deflect the driver's attention. "Yeah, thanks a heap, mister. We've had a rough patch of luck lately."

"We're making a fresh start." Trisha lifted her shirt, exposing a pink bra and washboard abs. She rubbed her flat stomach. "For the little one."

The driver ignored the blatant display of skin, and Trisha ignored Rake's pleading eyes.

"Speaking of which, you mind if I pee?" She smirked as she held up a grease-smeared funnel and an empty soda bottle. She must have found them in the back of the van.

"We were just at a rest stop!" Rake looked to the driver for backup.

"Tell that to the rugrat playing kickball with my bladder." Trisha dangled the funnel, waiting for an answer.

"Just don't spill any," the driver said.

"*No problemo*. I'm a pro."

Trisha turned her back and put a hand on the rear seat for balance. Then she dropped her panties to her ankles and squatted, exposing half her ass in the process. Rake couldn't help but watch.

"She ain't shy," he said to the driver as the bottle filled. The driver kept his eyes glued to the road. Not even a passing glance in the mirror.

Trisha looked over her shoulder and gave Rake a quizzical look. He shrugged. Trisha finished her business and hiked her panties back up. She capped the bottle and set it on the floor.

Go on she motioned to Rake. *Your turn*. He ran a nervous tongue across his lips. He hated this part, but he couldn't say no to her, especially after her little display. He never could.

"What about you?" Rake said, turning back to the driver.

"What's your, uh... story?" He put his hand on the driver's thigh.

The driver looked down at Rake's hand, then slowly looked up at his eyes. Trisha watched in stunned silence as the driver held the gaze, ignoring the road. The van's alignment must have been spot-on, because if they weren't on a straightaway, it would have careened off the interstate. After a small eternity the driver turned back to the road with the same lack of urgency.

"I'm not much for conversation."

Rake looked back at Trisha in disbelief.

"Just trying to be personable is all."

"Don't make an effort on my account." The driver patted the engine housing. "This baby does enough talking for both of us."

Rake leaned back in his seat and stared out the window, his stomach a queasy mix of rejection and relief. The yellow of the setting sun pulled thin across the cloudless horizon. What had he learned back in school? The fewer particles that were in the atmosphere for light to interact with, the fewer colors you'd see in the sky. The lack of red and orange reminded Rake of how far they were from industrious civilization.

He turned to the driver to give it another go, only to find the face of an alien staring back at him, his own surprise reflected in its large black eyes. He looked on in shock as the alien reached out a human hand and flipped a switch under the dashboard. Exhaust poured out of the vents.

"What the hell?"

Trisha was already on her feet, revolver trained on the driver. It took Rake a moment to realize the man wore a gas mask. He reached for the window crank, but it wouldn't budge.

"I told you," the driver said, his voice distorted by the mask, "window don't work."

"Pull over, now!" Trisha pressed the gun against the driver's head. Rake threw his shoulder into the passenger window.

Trisha pulled back the hammer. "Pull over or I shoot." The driver didn't flinch.

"Are you crazy?" Rake pushed the gun away from the driver, coughing. "You'll kill us all!"

"You got a better idea?"

"Shoot the fucking window!"

Trisha turned her upper body 45 degrees and fired. A hertzian cone the size of a quarter appeared in the glass. Rake slammed his fist against the window, panicking. He pressed his mouth over the hole and sucked air.

'You trying to get shot in the face?" Trisha grabbed his shoulder and pulled him away from the window. A sliver of glass protruded from his lip.

"I can't fucking breathe!"

Trisha raised the gun to shoot again.

The driver pumped the brakes, hard, just as the weapon discharged. Trisha flew forward over the engine housing, slamming her head into the dashboard. The shot hit Rake in the thigh. The tires screeched and the van fishtailed, a hundred feet of blacktop flying by in the span of a second, before the driver floored the accelerator and sent Trisha's unconscious body flying into the back.

Rake clutched his bleeding leg, drawing shallow breaths. He became acutely aware of the tiny molecules of carbon monoxide binding with his hemoglobin, restricting his oxygen supply. *I can't believe it,* he thought as he passed out. *Shot twice in one week. I should have stayed in school.*

Part Two

[Nobody Rides For Free is filmed before a live studio audience]

Trisha comes to, one eye at a time, her vision a haze of dark cotton. Cotton that must be in her mouth and ears as well, because her hearing is muffled and her tongue feels thick. In fact, it feels like her whole head is packed with the stuff, her thoughts getting caught in the tangle of gauzy fiber. She wants to reach up and pull it out, like her head is a newly-opened bottle of aspirin, but her arms are tied behind her back.

She sits up and blinks, the darkness murmuring around her. Her ankles are also bound. Next to her, what appears to be a potato sack emits a quiet groan.

"Rake?" Trisha shifts her weight, shimmies over to him.

"What's happening? Where are we?"

"I don't know. Are you okay?"

"You fucking shot me. Of course I'm not okay."

"That bastard driver got the jump on us. Here, let me see if I can untie you."

Trisha rolls her body over his, so they lay back to back.

"Shit. I think it's a zip tie. We'll have to find some way to cut it." She rocks her body up into a kneeling position. "You stay here. I'm gonna have a look around."

Trisha inch-worms to her feet, but before she can hop off into the darkness, there is a drag and a sputter and then an engine roars to life.

[Cue engine]

A whimper catches in her throat as she pictures a man in a dead skin mask wielding a giant chainsaw. The blade is six feet long and powered by a Slant 6. She flashes back to the Dodge A100, the last thing she remembers before waking up in this nightmare.

"Trisha!" Rake yells.

[Cue lights]

A pair of halogen lamps switch on, momentarily blinding them. Four more follow in succession, filling the area with light. Extension cords snake away from each, plugging into a rumbling generator. Rotting wooden walls rise high above them. Dirt and hay cover the floor.

The first thing Rake does as his eyes adjust is look down at his thigh. The wound has been cleaned and dressed. Same goes for his foot. The next thing he notices is another human being, hogtied on the floor next to him. Desperate eyes plead for Rake's help. There is a crackle and some feedback, and then a silhouette to the left of them shouts through a megaphone.

[Cut to C Camera]

"Good evening, ladies and gentlemen. Does everybody know what time it is?" A crowd roars in the affirmative. Trisha doesn't understand how that is possible. The silhouette nods its head. "That's right, it's time for another exciting game of Nobody Rides For Free!"

[Cue music, APPLAUSE sign; cut to A Camera]

A bluegrass three-piece off to the right launches into a chicken-pickin' shuffle. Rake tenses as hoots and hollers buffet him from the dark. He can barely make out a crowd of people sitting in a section of portable bleachers, like at a sporting event. He squints at the shadow with the megaphone. It is the driver of the A100.

[Cut to B Camera, Master Shot]

"What the hell's going on?" Trisha says to the man, mustering as much authority as she can. It comes out more like: *please sir, can I have some more?*

"Time to settle up, miss."

"We have money."

Mr. A100 chuckles. "That's not what your buddy Rake here said back at the truck stop."

"We do. Lots of it. In the dufflebag. If you just let me go back to the—"

"Let me stop you right there." Mr. A100 kicks the open duffle bag into the light. The revolver sits atop a bed of cash. "It's too late for that. There's only one way to settle this, and you know what that is?" He cups a hand around his ear and turns in the direction of the crowd, which chants: *Ass, gas, or grass! Ass, gas, or grass! Ass, gas, or grass! Ass, gas, or grass!*

The chanting continues as Rake and Trisha look on, confused. The third captive whimpers into the dirt. Mr. A100 walks over to a six-foot ghost made of dingy drop cloth.

"That's right, we let the wheel decide." He pulls away the

cloth to reveal a rickety carnival wheel. The wheel is divided into six sections like a pie, each one painted with one of three words: *ass*, *gas*, or *grass*.

"Let me show you how this works."

[Cue Stagehand]

Mr. A100 motions to the third captive and a—farmhand? Stagehand?—appears to deliver a swift kick to the man's ribs.

"Spin the wheel, fucker."

The captive shuffles to the wheel on his knees, drooling and blubbering. He grasps one of the wooden dowels lining its perimeter with his teeth. He looks to Mr. A100 for reassurance.

"Go on," Mr. A100 says.

[Close-up on man]

The man snaps his neck to spin the wheel, multicolored wedges blending into a swirl of brown. The other captives look on in horror. The crowd holds its breath. The clicking of the dowels against the flapper slows until finally the wheel comes to a stop.

"Ass it is!" Mr. A100 says through the megaphone. The crowd erupts with approval.

[Cue Dominatrix]

A curvaceous blonde neck-deep in black latex struts out on six-inch stiletto heels. The audience cat-calls and wolf-whistles. Flashing a performer's smile she caresses the cheek of the whimpering man. Her touch brings hope welling up in his eyes. Perhaps she is a shiny black angel, there to deliver him from his suffering.

But that hope is dashed as she dons a twelve-inch strap-on and subjects him to a vicious sodomizing, much to the crowd's delight.

[Cut to Commercial]

———

The man's horrific screaming led Officer Pendleton to the barn. She had all but given up after the A100 turned down the pitch-black farm road. She had driven past, then doubled back and killed the lights to ensure she wouldn't be seen, which felt like driving into hell blind. Eventually she had to stop the car and walk, just to be sure she didn't give herself away. Things were already in full swing when she finally caught up, over an hour later. With no idea how to proceed she just watched through the slats as some poor man was violated, face down in the dirt. That's when the doubt kicked in.

What the hell was she doing here, putting her life and career on the line? She'd never even liked Ramirez. They barely got along. Not to mention the incident in the locker room with the deli meat...

But no—like him or not, he had been her partner, and he deserved justice. As did the rest of the officers injured at Bellamy. She was here because it was the right thing to do, even if it meant disobeying a direct order. She turned back to the action and started to formulate a plan.

———

[Return]

The stagehand pushes Rake towards the wheel. He winces as the muscle tissue in his injured quad screams.

"Your turn." Mr. A100 smiles.

Rake looks to the Dominatrix as she lifts herself off the other man—who has collapsed in silence—and then back to Trisha. He usually followed her lead when shit went splat, but for once she seems out of ideas.

"We don't got all night, son," he hears Mr. A100 say. Another stagehand drags the other captive away. It is unclear whether he is alive or dead.

Rake grips a dowel with his teeth, trying to maintain eye contact with Trisha. Just in case she has some last minute inspiration and he is given a reprieve. The action feels involuntary as he spins the wheel.

"Round and round she goes." Mr. A100 says it in a lilting

sing-song. The crowd dials down to a low murmur as the clicking wheel slows.

Assgasgrassassgasgrassassgasgrassassgasgrass...

The wheel comes to a stop.

[Close-up on Wheel]

"Oh, come on!" Rake turns to Mr. A100 in protest.

"Looks like ass again!" The crowd roars. The dominatrix strokes her glistening cock.

Rake pleads his case as the stagehand drags him towards his doom. "Wait! You can't do this!"

"Just try to relax," Trisha calls out. "Like that time with the drag queen."

Rake ignores her. "Please, I didn't get a good grip. Let me spin again!"

Mr. A100 holds up his hand to silence the crowd.

"Are you saying you want to double down, son?"

"Yes! Anything! Please!"

"You hear that, folks?" Mr. A100 turns to the crowd with a flourish. "We've got ourselves a high roller. Man wants to double down on *ass*!"

[Cue Wheel #2]

The crowd roars as another stagehand brings out a second wheel and whips off its cloth. It has twice as many wedges. For every one marked *gas* or *grass*, there are two marked *ass*.

"What the hell, man?" Rake struggles against his bonds as a stagehand drags him towards the new wheel. He looks to Trisha, who can only watch in horror. Mr. A100 casually checks his watch.

The stagehand positions Rake in front of the wheel. Forces the dowel into his mouth like a man about to have his leg amputated. When Rake does nothing, the stagehand rocks him back and forth, building up momentum, and then pushes forward with all his might, throwing Rake face first into the dirt in the process. The wheel clicks, double-time. Rake stays face down. He can't bear to look. He prays as the clicks slow, until finally they stop.

Amen, he says to himself.

[Close-up on Wheel]

"Gas!" Mr. A100's voice crackles through the megaphone.

Nervous laughter escapes Rake's lungs. "That's good, right? Gas is good?" He looks over at Trisha who smiles through her tears, nodding her head, willing it to be.

"It sure is," Mr. A100 says. "Especially when it's combined with ASS!"

[Cue Stagehands]

The crowd screams even louder than before. Rake stares in shock as two more stagehands hold him down. One pulls his pants to his knees while the other greases a length of clear tubing attached to a funnel, possibly the same one Trisha used to urinate in the van.

Before he can protest, the stagehand roughly forces the tube inside him. Rake's eyes bulge and the veins in his neck pop as he screams. At least a foot's worth of hose disappears inside his body. Then the stagehand pours a gallon can of gasoline into the funnel.

"That's good, boys," Mr. A100 says. "Make sure he takes every drop."

Rake turns green almost instantly. He clenches his stomach and starts to retch. Viscous amber liquid leaks from his mouth. One of the stagehands notices and clamps a hand over it. Rake's body continues to heave as the other stagehand shakes the last few drops of gasoline into the funnel.

Trisha fights against her binding, screaming. "Let him go!"

"You heard the lady," says Mr. A100.

The stagehand yanks the hose from Rake's body. The other releases his mouth. Gasoline sprays from both ends. When it is over he lies shivering in the remnants of his fossil fuel enema.

"And that, ladies and gentlemen, is the way the wheel wobbles. Somebody bring this man a towel."

One of the stagehands wraps a towel around Rake's shoulders and helps him over to Trisha. He crumples into her. Trisha nuzzles him as best she can. "Sh... it's all over, baby. Just try to relax."

Mr. Aɪoo smiles at the heartwarming scene. "You've fulfilled your obligation to the wheel, my friend. You are free to go."

"I—I am?"

"Sure as shittin'."

"What about Trisha?"

"Trisha, unfortunately, still owes a debt to the wheel. Unless, of course, you want to step up like a man and take the lady's turn?"

Trisha stiffens. She stares at the cold justice of the wheel.

Rake goes into convulsions at the mere mention of more.

"I... I can't. Can't take anymore."

"You sure?" says Mr. Aɪoo. "Like I said, you're free to walk out of here, but you're not likely to make it very far. Even as we speak, that gasoline is rotting through your insides. Won't be long before your throat closes, your blood pressure drops, and you collapse. Surprised you lasted this long."

[Tight on Rake and Trisha]

Rake looks up at Trisha.

"Please... don't make me..."

Trisha looks away. "But if it means the chance of one of us making it out of here alive..."

"Trisha, please..."

She places a hand on her stomach. "What about... the little one?"

Rake stops shaking. "You're pregnant for real?"

Trisha nods her head.

"Is it mine?"

She looks him in the eye. "You would have raised it either way, right?"

A tear trickles from the corner of said eye. A single, clear rivulet that becomes diluted by dirt and gasoline the further it travels down his cheek. He attempts a smile. Only half his face complies.

"Anything for you, Sis."

And then the convulsions kick back in. Rake coughs up blood and phlegm, spraying it everywhere. Trisha scrunches up her face to protect her eyes. When she opens them Rake is dead.

[Cut to B Camera, Master]

"Looks like the decision's been made." Mr. A100 says it with the solemnity of a funeral director. It is the eye of his storm of showmanship. He moves the megaphone away from his mouth and leans towards Trisha. "And just for the record, we know you ain't pregnant. Remember that bottle of piss from the van? Had one of the boys run down to the pharmacy for some dip-sticks. We like our fun, but we ain't animals." He turns back to the crowd, enthusiasm going from zero to sixty. "Let's bring out another wheel!"

[Cue APPLAUSE sign, Wheel #3]

Trisha's face melts in an expression of Munchian dread. The stagehands escort out another drop-clothed wheel.

"What's it gonna be?" Mr. A100 whips off the cloth to reveal the new "prizes." The audience shouts them out.

[Close-up on Wheel #3]

Mutts, butts, or guts! Mutts, butts, or guts!

[Cue music, Cut to A Camera]

The band kicks into another uptempo number. A stagehand manhandles Trisha in the direction of the wheel. The thick-necked youth has to guide her mouth to a dowel, she's shaking so much. She closes her eyes as she bites down and prepares to learn her fate.

"Let's show the lady what she'll be playing for, shall we?"

[Cue spotlight, Cut to C Camera]

Mr. A100 gestures to his right. Another work lamp switches on, illuminating the three options: a man restraining two snarling dogs, a woman in a three-piece suit smoking a cigar, and another man turning a hand-held crank that spins a miniature wheel of hooks.

[Cue APPLAUSE sign]

The crowd shows all three an equal amount of love, but

their adulation is cut short by a skirmish as a stagehand drags someone new out onto the floor.

[Cue Stagehand, New Contestant]

"But what's this, ladies and gentlemen, there seems to be a new player joining the game." Mr. A100 shoots a glance off-stage, to where a middle-aged man dressed like a network executive watches the proceedings.

A stagehand drops a hot potato sack of woman roughly on the ground. She wears a brown uniform. The stagehand dusts off his hands and spits.

"Found this bitch sneaking around outside." He hands Mr. A100 a 9mm pistol. "Think she's a cop."

"Show some respect, boy. That's a *lady* cop." Mr. A100 circles the crumpled woman, who glares from beneath her bangs. He toes her badge. "From Bellamy, apparently."

[Close-up on Trisha]

"To what do we owe the pleasure?" Mr. A100 maintains his professional demeanor.

"Official police business." Officer Pendleton drills eye-holes in Trisha.

"Little bit out of your jurisdiction, isn't it?"

She doesn't respond.

"I see. It's personal." Mr. A100 looks over at Trisha. "You wouldn't happen to know anything about this, would you?"

Trisha shakes her head, avoids looking at Officer Pendleton.

"You sure?" Mr. A100 looks over to The Executive again. The man gives a slight nod.

Trisha looks from Mr. A100 to the cop, but says nothing.

"This about that shit that went down at the Motor Lodge?" Mr. A100 says. "Heard about that mess. You think they'd send a whole task force after the maniacs what perpetrated that blood bath. Where's your backup, Officer?"

"They're right behind me."

Mr. A100 scans her face. "Even if you didn't have rogue written all over you, they'd be hours away. We'll be long gone by then."

"You're all under arrest. You need to return my gun, and remand the fugitive into my custody."

"Ha!" Mr. A100's staccato laugh punctuates the silence. "That's not going to happen. At least not before the young lady spins the wheel."

"I need to take her back unharmed."

"Well then maybe you want to spin the wheel for her?"

Both Officer Pendleton and Trisha's eyes widen. Mr. A100 turns to the audience. "How about it? Should we let the officer pinch-spin?"

The audience erupts into mean-spirited cheers, exhibiting no love for the law. The Executive continues to watch.

"Looks like the ayes have it."

A stagehand pushes Trisha out of the way while another tosses Officer Pendleton in front of the wheel.

"Spin," Mr. A100 says, away from the megaphone, flecks of spittle giving the word an added menace.

Officer Pendleton surveys the three possibilities. The dogs pull at their handler, red rockets at the ready. The woman in the suit puffs out her chest as she puffs her cigar. The third person turns his crank, the rusty hooks rotating like a demented Ferris wheel. The officer turns back to Mr. A100.

"No."

The stagehand kicks her square between the shoulder blades. Her body jerks forward, head catching one of the dowels on the wheel before it meets the ground with a thud. The wheel spins.

[Cue APPLAUSE sign]

Newton's first law remains constant as the wheel slows down. The clicking of the dowels becomes fewer and farther between. *Mutts, butts, guts, mutts, butts, guts... mutts... butts... guts... mutts...*

The momentum of the wheel slows to a crawl. The dogs froth and growl. The audience leans forward in their seats.

Click.

[Close-up on Wheel]

The wheel stops at *butts*.

Roars of approval fill the silence. The smoking woman grins, the cherry of the cigar glowing red as she steps forward. A pair of stagehands restrains Officer Pendleton, who stares down the approaching woman. She leans in, touches her nose to the cop's, and exhales smoke in her face. Officer Pendleton sputters.

[Close-up on Officer Pendleton]

"Don't worry, sugar. Butts ain't the same as ass." The smoking woman brings the cigar down towards the cop's neck. Trisha turns away.

Flesh sizzles and a scream fills the air. But it doesn't come from Officer Pendleton. It comes from Trisha, her eyes scrunched tight. Officer Pendleton tenses and grunts with each burn, but doesn't give the audience the satisfaction of screaming. When the ordeal is through, Mr. Aroo initiates a slow clap.

[Cut to C Camera]

"*Very* impressive. I admire your restraint. You may live through this yet. What do you say, audience? Give the officer a nice round of applause."

The crowd begrudgingly responds with a smattering of claps and grumbles. Officer Pendleton lays exhausted on the ground, angry red dots peppering her face and arms.

Mr. Aroo turns to Trisha. "Looks like you're off the hook, miss. Your debt's been paid." He turns to the recuperating cop. "One of them at least."

The audience voices their disapproval.

"I know, I know..." Mr. Aroo says. "But rules are rules. We follow the law of the wheel, whether we like it or not. Officer, I remand the fugitive into your custody."

Officer Pendleton staggers to her feet. "My gun."

"Sorry, Officer, no can do. That's one for the loss column."

Officer Pendleton nods, grabs Trisha by the wrists and lifts her to her feet. She gives one last look at the audience before leading her suspect towards the barn door. The audience watches them go in silence.

[Cut to B Camera, Master]

"Wait!" Trisha pulls at her captor and turns back towards the crowd. "Wait! I want to double down!"

The crowd murmurs in excitement. Mr. A100 glances at The Executive.

"Let me get this straight. You want to double down... on freedom?"

Trisha pushes against Officer Pendleton some more. "This ain't freedom. I'd rather take my chances with the wheel."

Mr. A100 makes a show of thinking about it. "I'm afraid there's technically nothing for you to double down on. You never actually spun the wheel."

"Then give me a chance. Please. I don't want to go out like this. I'm a player. I want to play the game."

"Well..." Mr. A100 surveys the audience. They are at the edge of their seats. "We could institute a bonus round."

"Bullshit," says Officer Pendleton. "I won fair and square. We're going."

Two stagehands restrain the women.

"Now just wait a minute. A bonus round isn't unheard of. It wouldn't be against the rules. Audience?"

It is the question they have been waiting for. Their answer is unanimous.

[Cut to A Camera]

"Well alright then. Bonus round it is!" The band kicks into another upbeat number as the crowd cheers.

[Cut to Commercial]

————

[Return]

Three new wheels crowd the stage, each covered in drop cloth.

"Here are the rules," Mr. A100 says. "We flip a coin to see who goes first. The winner picks a wheel and spins. Because this is a bonus round, that person has the option of passing and spinning again. If this happens, the second contestant must accept the first prize. There is no doubling down. Have you understood the rules as I've explained them to you?"

Both women nod in the affirmative.

"So be it." Mr. Aioo reaches into his pocket and produces a shiny silver dollar. He brandishes it in front of the contestants. "As you can see, this is not a trick coin. It features both a head and a tail. Trisha, would you like to call it?"

"Heads."

"Heads it is." Mr. Aioo positions the coin atop his thumbnail and flicks it into the air. End over end it spins, glinting in the light of the worklamps. The audience's collective intake of breath sucks the air from the room. The coin falls to the dirt with a thud. Both contestants lean in to view the results.

[Close-up of coin]

"Tails," Mr. Aioo says.

"Works for me," says Trisha, her game face on.

"Well..." Mr. Aioo turns toward Officer Pendleton. "Which will it be?"

The audience calls out as the cop weighs her options. There are equal calls for *one*,

two, and *three*, mixing together to form a numerical fugue.

Mr. Aioo turns to Pendleton. "You don't have to listen to them. Go with your heart."

Officer Pendleton's lips move, forming a single word. Mr. Aioo holds up his hand, silencing the audience.

"I'm sorry, what was that?"

"I said two."

Mr. Aioo brings the megaphone to his lips.

"The officer has chosen! Wheel *numero dos*!"

The crowd does its thing.

[Cut to C Camera]

"Now before we decide your ultimate fate, let's see what might have been." Mr. Aioo walks over to the first wheel, pulls off the cloth with a flourish. The guitar player plucks a familiar banjo lick as the crowd groans in dismay.

"*Fam*, *clam,* or *spam*. An audience favorite."

"I like spam!" a spectator calls out in a high-pitched voice.

Mr. A100 smiles. "I know you do." He walks over to the third wheel. "And let's see what's behind door number three!" He pulls off the cloth.

Aaaaaaaaaaaw...

"*Cleet*, *skeet*, or *feet*. Another popular one." He approaches the middle wheel. "And then there was one. You guys ready?"

The crowd cheers. Mr. A100 turns to Officer Pendleton, moves the megaphone away from his face. "Are *you* ready?"

He doesn't wait for an answer. He whisks the cloth away and the crowd gasps. Officer Pendleton takes in the wheel. It contains two words that in any other situation would seem benign. But painted on the wheel, those words are a death sentence. The third word, however, the third word inspires hope. Hope that she might actually make it out of this alive.

[Close-up on Wheel]

"Very interesting, veeeeeery interesting indeed." Mr. A100 paces back and forth in front of the crowd. "Such a tantalizing word, that last one. So many possibilities. I wonder what it could mean." He turns back to the audience, unable to suppress his enthusiasm. "Let's find out, shall we?"

[Cut to C Camera]

"We have... *hawk*..." Mr. A100 points. A stagehand in a medieval tunic stands there, a large, hooded bird of prey resting on his outstretched arm. "*Caulk*..." Mr. A100 points to a handyman in overalls wielding a caulk gun. "Or..." Mr. A100 spins in a circle, a human carnival wheel, until his index finger finally comes to rest on the open door of the barn. "*Walk*."

A reverent hush falls over the crowd.

"That's right, *walk*. What you are free to do if the wheel so decides."

Mr. A100 stares into Officer Pendleton's eyes. There is hope there, but the rest of her body is unsure.

"Do you mean it?"

"Sure do, miss. The word of the wheel is law, and we abide by that law."

"What about her?" She motions towards Trisha.

"She would still have to spin the wheel."

Officer Pendleton looks towards the door. A hint of pink enters the horizon.

"It's almost morning, and the game's almost done. Would you care to spin?" Mr. A100 holds out a hand towards the wheel.

Officer Pendleton steps up and grasps a dowel. She casts one last look at the audience, out of the corner of her eye. They look like normal people, not blood-thirsty voyeurs. It makes her think of Bellamy. The male suspect was dead, but she had a chance to bring his accomplice to justice.

And then she spins.

Clickclickclickclickclickclickclickclickclickclickclickclickclickclickclickclick

The blur of letters has a hypnotic effect. As the wheel slows and the stripes of color separate into actual words, a wave of calm washes over Officer Pendleton. She is still lost in that calm when the wheel comes to a stop. The crowd gasps.

[Close-up on Wheel]

"I don't believe my eyes, ladies and gentlemen. The wheel has seen fit to let the officer *walk*."

Disbelief ripples through the crowd. The handyman slumps in disappointment. The hooded hawk flaps its wings.

"Caw!"

Officer Pendleton's vision focuses on the four white letters. They indeed spell *walk*. Her relief comes out in a mixture of laughter and tears. Trisha curses up a streak.

"You are a very lucky lady." Mr. A100 places the megaphone in her hand. "Why don't you tell the audience how you feel?"

Officer Pendleton looks over at Trisha. This was a type of justice, wasn't it? A much harsher one than she'd face at the hands of the law. All Pendleton had to do was walk away. Ramirez would be avenged and she'd get to live. She might even make it to her psych evaluation. She didn't know how she'd explain the pepperoni-sized burns all over her face, but still. She turns back to the audience.

"My turn's not over." Her arms hang limp by her side. "I pass."

"I'm sorry, I don't think the audience heard you." Mr. Aioo guides her arm, the megaphone towards her mouth. She presses the button.

"I said I pass."

A squelch of feedback punctuates the statement. The audience's collective intake of breath threatens to turn their bodies inside out. For once, Mr. Aioo is at a loss for words.

But Trisha isn't.

"You heard the bitch!" Her voice fills the room as she gets to her feet. "I'm gettin' the fuck outta here!"

There are scattered coughs and throat clears from the audience. Mr. Aioo looks hurt. He turns to The Executive, then to Officer Pendleton. He finds his tongue.

"We've been waiting all night for this bitch to spin the wheel. Why would you do that?"

Officer Pendleton is steely in her resolve. "I need her alive."

"You realize that you also need to *be* alive to bring her to justice, right? You already survived one round, which is a fucking miracle."

"If I don't bring her to justice, someone else will. And if by some chance I do make it out of this alive..." She finishes her sentence with a stare that could melt glass, stopping Trisha's celebration in its tracks.

"Is this really what you want?" Mr. Aioo asks. He almost seems concerned.

"It is."

Mr. Aioo grabs the brim of his hat, uses the back of the same hand to wipe his brow.

"So be it."

He nods towards Trisha.

"Cut her loose."

The stagehands comply. Trisha stands there, rubbing the circulation back into her wrists.

"I don't suppose I get my money back?"

"That money was never yours," Mr. Aroo says.

Trisha nods. She walks over to Rake's expired body and crouches down beside him. She touches two fingers to her lips and presses them against his. They are already cold to the touch.

"I'm sorry."

She turns and walks slowly from the barn. She can feel the eyes of Officer Pendleton, Mr. Aroo, and the entire audience watching her. Even a hundred yards from the barn, under the warming morning sky, all she can hear is birdsong. She has no car and no money, but her thumb still works and the breeze feels nice. She looks like shit, but when did that ever matter? She tilts her head back and closes her eyes, and continues walking in what she assumes is the direction of the road.

Finally, a cheer goes up from the barn behind her, followed by the tell-tale clicking of the wheel. When the wheel finally stops, the crowd goes bug-shit.

Trisha breaks into a run.

[Cue music, roll credits]

STORY NOTES

LETTERS TO THE PURPLE SATIN KILLER

Originally published in Thuglit #20, November 2015
This story was inspired by the true crime documentary,
Making a Murderer. Specifically, the bit where Steven Avery
becomes engaged to Sandy Greenman while serving a life
sentence in jail.

It got me thinking about women who reach out to men in
prison, and prison letters in general. I thought it would be
interesting to tell the story of an inmate completely from
the perspective of the letters they receive. It earned me a
coveted spot in Thuglit, not long before they closed shop.

In fact, a pretty reputable agent reached out to me as a
direct result. He asked if I had anything else, so I sent him
the first fifty pages of a novel I was working on. He said
while he admired the ingenuity of the thing, no agent would
ever take it on. Luckily CLASH doesn't care about agents or
their opinions. They'll be putting the book out in 2020.

TWICE AMPUTATED FOOT

Originally published at Zetetic: A Record of Unusual Inquiry, June 2015

My first published story. Also my most personal, although I hid the details under a bunch of weird crap, just like I do with my feelings!

THE BLACK HOLE

Originally published at Fabula Argentea, June 2015

This is what I would call a sciency fiction story. It's got science in it, but it's not a straight-up genre piece. And no, it wasn't influenced by *Interstellar*. At the time of this story's writing I had yet to see said film. Lucky for you, dear reader, the story's a lot shorter.

HOMUNCULOID

Originally published at Motherboard (Vice), June 2015

My second published story. Also my first pro sale (and last for quite a while. Don't get cocky, kids!) This was originally written for and rejected by a videogame anthology that never materialized. I have no recollection of where the initial idea came from. It started weird and got weirder from there. It's written in the format of one of those old *How to Win at Nintendo Games* books, as dictated by the original call.

MAISON D'OEUFS

Originally published in Unnerving Magazine #1, December 2016
The idea for this story started with a title I didn't use: *Life Begins at Delicious*. I'm still partial to that one, but felt it telegraphed the ending, so I went with something a little

subtler. Proud the story appeared in the inaugural issue of what has gone on to be a great market for horror fiction.

MUMMER'S PARADE

Originally published in *Final Masquerade* (Lycan Valley Press), October 2016

I discovered what a mummer was reading George R.R. Martin's Song of Ice and Fire series. He kept using the term "mummer's farce", and it prompted me to do a little research. I read quite a bit about Philadelphia, racially insensitive costumes, and a fella named *Zwarte Piet*, none of which made it into the story. Still, I feel the research helped inform the final product.

THE HAND OF GOD

Originally published in Dark Moon Digest #21, October 2015

This story started with the line, "He could feel the hand of God, fingers wrapped tight around his throat," and it went from there. This is another personal one—as personal as a story about being possessed by God can be.

SUPREME MATHEMATICS: A CIPHER

Originally published in *This Book Ain't Nuttin to Fuck With: A Wu-Tang Tribute Anthology* (CLASH Books), January 2017

The first line of this story was inspired by an image from the Jason Banker/Amy Everson film, *Felt*. (Do yourself a favor and check that one out.) That's all I had for a while, and I didn't know what to do with it until I joined forces with the Wu. Their devotion to Kung Fu movies and the Five-Percent Nation informed the rest of the piece.

WHISPERS IN THE EAR OF A DREAMING APE

Originally published in Janus: Pantheon Magazine #11, August 2017

The titular story of the collection. This was like the fourth or fifth suggestion, but once the decision was made it became obvious it was perfect. Because that's what stories are, right? This marked my second appearance in a Pantheon publication, and it was just as thrilling as the first.

THE WHOLE INFERNAL MACHINE

Originally published in Kzine #18, May 2017

This is the first story I completed after committing to writing and submitting "for realsies." It was rejected *fifty times* before being accepted by Kzine. And then—I don't think many people read it. So I'm excited for it to get a second life in this collection.

AFT LAVATORY OCCUPIED

Originally published in The Wyrd #2, April 2019

Another one that started with the title. I came up with it— you guessed it—on a plane. But I had no idea what the story would be about.

A while later I came across a Stephen King anecdote. I think it was in *Dans Macabre* or *On Writing*, but don't hold me to that. It was about this story idea he had. About a bathroom (I remember it being on a plane or in an airport) that people kept going into and never coming out of. Eventually they sent in law enforcement, then the army, but no one ever returned. Was it a portal to another dimension?

King said he never wrote it because he had no idea how it ended. So I finished it for him. (Kind of but not really, please don't sue.)

THE GOSPEL OF X

New to this collection

I had an idea to write a story in what I would call "Biblical" format. Chapters, verses, quotations in red. A kind of new New Testament. I combined that with a *Hellraiser*-meets-Ken-Russell's-*The-Devils* idea and *voila*! No one wanted it. Hence—new to this collection. I've been waiting to unleash this bad boy on the world since August 2016.

NOBODY RIDES FOR FREE

Originally published in Dark Moon Digest #31, April 2018

I decided I was going to write a story based on the old bumper sticker, "Ass, gas, or grass." And that's just what I did. Somehow, it evolved into a sort of *Deliverance* meets Wheel of Fortune hybrid, with stage directions like a script for a multi-camera show. My second time in DMD. Who else was gonna accept this story but Max and Lori?

ACKNOWLEDGMENTS

I would like to thank all the original publishers for fostering these bastard children of mine. My wife Rebekah, for being my first reader, always. Christoph and Leza for saying yes. The members of the LitReactor Writers Workshop, where many of these stories were incubated and refined. And finally, to all the friends and family who bought this book with the hopes of seeing their names listed here. Suckers.

ABOUT THE AUTHOR

Joshua Chaplinsky is the Managing Editor of LitReactor.-com. He is the author of 'Kanye West—Reanimator.' His short fiction has been published by Motherboard, Vol. 1 Brooklyn, Thuglit, Severed Press, Perpetual Motion Machine Publishing, Pantheon Magazine, and Broken River Books. Follow him on Twitter at @jaceycockrobin. More info at joshuachaplinsky.com.

ALSO BY CLASH BOOKS

TRAGEDY QUEENS: STORIES INSPIRED BY LANA DEL REY & SYLVIA PLATH

Edited by Leza Cantoral

GIRL LIKE A BOMB

Autumn Christian

CENOTE CITY

Monique Quintana

99 POEMS TO CURE WHATEVER'S WRONG WITH YOU OR CREATE THE PROBLEMS YOU NEED

Sam Pink

THIS BOOK IS BROUGHT TO YOU BY MY STUDENT LOANS

Megan J. Kaleita

PAPI DOESN'T LOVE ME NO MORE

Anna Suarez

ARSENAL/SIN DOCUMENTOS

Francesco Levato

THIS IS A HORROR BOOK

Charles Austin Muir

FOGHORN LEGHORN

Big Bruiser Dope Boy

TRY NOT TO THINK BAD THOUGHTS

Art by Matthew Revert

SEQUELLAND
Jay Slayton-Joslin

JAH HILLS
Unathi Slasha

HEXIS
Charlene Elsby

I'M FROM NOWHERE
Lindsay Lerman

NEW VERONIA
M.S. Coe

SPORTSCENTER POEMS
Poetry by Christoph Paul & Art by Jim Agpalza

DARK MOONS RISING IN A STARLESS NIGHT
Mame Bougouma Diene

NIGHTMARES IN ECSTASY
Brendan Vidito

THE ANACHIST KOSHER COOKBOOK
Maxwell Bauman

THE MUMMY OF CANAAN
Maxwell Bauman

TRASH PANDA
Leza Cantoral

THE HAUNTING OF THE PARANORMAL ROMANCE AWARDS
Christoph Paul & Mandy De Sandra

WE PUT THE LIT IN LITERARY

CL◢SH

CLASHBOOKS.COM

FOLLOW US ON TWITTER, IG & FB
@clashbooks

EMAIL
clashmediabooks@gmail.com

CPSIA information can be obtained
at www.ICGtesting.com
Printed in the USA
JSHW030825060420
4993JS00008B/765

9 781944 866587